# Sleepover Squad

#1 Sleeping Over

#2 Camping Out

#3 The Trouble With Brothers

#4 Keeping Secrets

Grab your pillow and join the

#1 *Sleeping Over*

#2 *Camping Out*

#3 *The Trouble with Brothers*

#4 *Keeping Secrets*

#5 *Pony Party!*

#6 *The New Girl*

# P. J. DENTON

# Sleepover Squad Collection

### #1 Sleeping Over
### #2 Camping Out
### #3 The Trouble With Brothers
### #4 Keeping Secrets

Illustrated by Julia Denos

ALADDIN PAPERBACKS

NEW YORK   LONDON   TORONTO   SYDNEY

ALADDIN

An imprint of Simon & Schuster Children's Publishing Division

1230 Avenue of the Americas, New York, NY 10020

*Sleeping Over* text copyright © 2007 by Catherine Hapka

*Sleeping Over* illustrations copyright © 2007 by Julia Denos

*Camping Out* text copyright © 2007 by Catherine Hapka

*Camping Out* illustrations copyright © 2007 by Julia Denos

*The Trouble with Brothers* text copyright © 2007 by Catherine Hapka

*The Trouble with Brothers* illustrations copyright © 2007 by Julia Denos

*Keeping Secrets* text copyright © 2008 by Catherine Hapka

*Keeping Secrets* illustrations copyright © 2008 by Julia Denos

All rights reserved, including the right of reproduction in whole or in part in any form.

ALADDIN and related logo

are registered trademarks of Simon & Schuster, Inc.

Designed by Karin Paprocki

The text of this book was set in Cochin.

The illustrations for this book were rendered in pen and ink.

Manufactured in the United States of America

0610 MTN

First Aladdin edition April 2009

2 4 6 8 10 9 7 5 3

Library of Congress Control Numbers

*Sleeping Over*: 2006927849

*Camping Out*: 2006928972

*The Trouble with Brothers*: 2006930151

*Keeping Secrets*: 2007937306

ISBN: 978-1-4169-9391-9

# P. J. DENTON

# Sleepover Squad

## #1 Sleeping Over

Illustrated by Julia Denos

# ✳ 1 ✳

## The First Day of the
## Last Week of School

"Happy first day of the last week of school!" Emily McDougal said as she walked into the kitchen of her family's old farmhouse. The kitchen was warm and steamy. It smelled like scrambled eggs and potting soil.

Emily's father was sitting at the kitchen table drinking tea and correcting tests. He liked to give the high school students he taught lots of tests. He told Emily it kept them on their toes.

"Thanks, Em," he said. His eyes were the same shade of blue as Emily's, and they crinkled at the corners when he smiled. "Want some eggs? I made French toast this morning too."

"Sure." Emily's stomach grumbled hungrily at the thought of her favorite breakfast. Her father usually had time to make French toast only on weekends.

Just then Emily's mother hurried into the kitchen. Mrs. McDougal hurried everywhere she went. That was how she made her organic plant and vegetable business so successful.

"Happy first day of the last week of school, Mommy," Emily said.

"Does that mean it's summer already?" Mrs. McDougal joked. "Oh no, I'm not ready!" She set the tray of cucumber seedlings she was carrying on the counter. Then she wiped her hands on her jeans and pushed back her wavy blond hair, which was sticking out around her face.

Mr. McDougal was busy fixing Emily a plate of eggs and French toast. "Pour yourself a glass of OJ, Em," he said. "Your mom and I want to talk to you about something before your bus gets here."

"Okay." Emily poured herself a glass of juice, then sat down. What did her parents want to talk about? They didn't look angry or disappointed, like they did when she

forgot to put away her clean laundry or scoop out her cat's litter box.

She didn't have long to wait. "The start of a new season seems like a perfect time for this," her mother announced, sitting down across from Emily. "After all, summer is a time of growth. Spring seedlings sprout up into healthy summer plants, baby animals get bigger and stronger as they explore their new world, all of nature blooms and grows and—"

"All right, Felicity," Mr. McDougal interrupted his wife with a smile. He tapped his wristwatch. "Em and I both need to get to school soon, you know."

"All right, all right," Emily's mother said. "Here's what we wanted to talk to you about, Emily. . . ."

Emily was still thinking about her talk with her parents when she got off the school bus outside Oak Tree Elementary.

She headed straight inside. As usual, her three best friends were waiting for her in the hallway outside their homeroom.

"Guess what?" she cried when she saw them.

"What?" Kara Wyatt asked immediately. Red-haired Kara was almost always the first one to speak up. She said it was because she had to be fast to get a word in around her four noisy brothers.

Meanwhile, Jo Sanchez peered at Emily. "Hey, you look weird," she said. "Is something wrong?"

That was just like Jo. She noticed things. And she was never afraid to ask about them.

Before she answered, Emily looked over at Taylor Kent to see whether she was paying attention. You never could be sure with Taylor. She always seemed to be trying to pay attention to four or five things at once.

This time, though, she was looking straight at Emily with curious, greenish gold eyes. "Well?" she said. "What's the big news, Emmers?"

Next Emily looked around to make sure nobody else was close enough to overhear. This kind of news was for the ears of her best friends alone. After all, they were the only ones in school who knew her embarrassing secret.

"You know my night-light?" she asked them in a quiet voice.

Kara, Jo, and Taylor nodded. Even though all four of them were in the second grade, only Emily still slept with a night-light in her bedroom. Her parents always said it was better that way, even though it made Emily feel like a baby.

"Sure. What about it?" Jo asked.

Emily took a deep breath. Then she smiled. "My parents just told me I can try sleeping without it," she announced. "They finally think I'm old enough."

Taylor gasped. "That's awesome!" she cried, grabbing Emily and hugging her. "Congratulations!"

Emily hugged her back. Over Taylor's shoulder she could see some of their classmates looking in their direction. Taylor's voice could be awfully loud. . . .

"Thanks," Emily said. She was glad her friends understood how important this was. "Don't tell anyone, though."

"Of course not," Kara promised. "We would never breathe a word about something like that."

Emily felt relieved. Her friends' assurances made her already great morning seem even better. "By the way, happy first day of the last week of school, you guys."

"*Gracias,*" Jo said. Emily knew that meant "thank you" in Spanish. Jo's whole family spoke Spanish at home sometimes, especially when her grandfather was visiting. "Same to you, Em," Jo added in English.

"Ooh, you're right—it's the last week of school!" Kara said, looking excited. "That means only a few more days until summer, summer, summer!"

Emily waited for Taylor to say something. But Taylor didn't seem to be paying attention anymore. She was staring down the hall with a faraway look on her face. Emily looked in the same direction, but she couldn't see anything except some third-grade boys giggling and snorting as they played keep-away with someone's baseball glove. There was nothing very interesting about that.

Kara noticed Taylor's faraway expression too. "Earth to Taylor!" she joked.

Taylor blinked, then turned to look at them. She ran one hand over her short, curly black hair. "Sorry," she said. "What were you guys saying?"

"It's the first day of the last week of school," Emily reminded her.

"Oh, I know," Taylor exclaimed, clapping her hands. "That reminds me—I haven't even told you guys my big news yet!"

"What big news?" Kara asked.

Just then the bell rang. It was time for everyone to go into homeroom and take their seats.

"Oops," Taylor said. "Guess I'll have to tell you later."

All morning long Taylor refused to spill her secret. "This is too big to tell in a hurry," she kept saying. "Just wait—I'll tell you at lunch."

For a while Emily thought lunchtime would never arrive. She could hardly wait to find out what Taylor wanted to tell them. Knowing Taylor, it had to be something fun!

Finally, the four friends were sitting in the cafeteria. They always sat at the same table—the small one in the corner near the windows overlooking the playground. That way, they could watch as all the other second and third graders headed outside for recess. Or they could eat in a hurry and rush outside themselves if they wanted.

"Are you going to tell us your big secret now, Taylor?" Kara asked the second she sat down. She tossed her lunch bag on the table without even opening it. "I'm dying of curiosity!"

Taylor grinned. "Really? You look like you're still alive to me," she teased.

"Taylor!" Kara cried, her voice rising to a squeak.

Jo rolled her eyes. "She's just trying to drive you crazy," she told Kara, carefully unpacking her usual lunch: a peanut butter sandwich, a bag of carrot sticks, and a chocolate chip cookie. "Come on, Taylor. You said you'd tell us your big news at lunch, and now it's lunch."

"Yes, please tell us!" Emily begged. "Pretty please!"

Taylor kept grinning. For a second Emily was afraid she would decide not to share after all. Taylor could be like that sometimes. She loved practical jokes and teasing almost as much as Kara's brothers did.

But then Taylor rested her elbows on

the table and leaned forward. "Okay," she said. "Here's my big news. My parents said I could have a party this Friday night to celebrate the start of summer vacation."

"Oh! That sounds like fun." Emily smiled. Taylor's parents sometimes let her have parties when it wasn't even her birthday. The last time had been on Valentine's Day, when Mr. and Mrs. Kent had taken Taylor and her friends to the ice-skating rink. They'd even had heart-shaped pizza for dinner at the snack bar.

"Cool," Kara added. "It's been ages since you had a party, Taylor."

"Oh, but you haven't even heard the best part yet. See, this isn't going to be an ordinary party." Taylor's eyes sparkled as she looked around at them. "It's a *sleepover* party. And you're all invited!"

# 2

## Taylor's Big Idea

"A sleepover party?" Kara cried. "Are you serious?"

"Wow!" Jo whistled. "That really *is* big news!"

Emily nodded slowly as her three friends continued chattering about Taylor's surprise. A sleepover—that wasn't just big news. It was huge news. Nobody in the second grade had ever had a slumber party before. But Emily had heard all about what fun sleepovers could be from her neighbor and babysitter, Courtney, who was fifteen.

"We can stay up late," Kara said eagerly. Her cheeks had gone almost as red as her hair, like they always did when she was excited. That made her freckles stand out even more.

"And we can play games like Truth or Dare and Whisper Down the Lane," Jo added.

Kara dumped her lunch out on the table. Her apple bounced across the table and off the edge onto the floor, but she didn't even notice. "And eat lots of junk food and watch scary movies on TV!" she said.

Taylor laughed, her eyes shining. "I knew you guys would love the idea," she exclaimed. "We're going to have the best time ever!"

Emily smiled along with the others. But secretly, she was worried. On the one hand, her friends were right—a sleepover sounded like lots of fun. On the other hand,

Emily's parents had just decided to let her unplug her night-light. Were they really going to let her sleep away from home?

"A last-day-of-school sleepover sounds great," she said. "But I have an even better idea. Why don't we have a picnic at my house instead? My dad can cook his famous garlic hot dogs on the grill, and we can play tag and stuff to welcome summer."

"Are you kidding?" Kara wrinkled her nose. "Picnics are nice, but what could possibly be more fun than a slumber party?"

Emily shrugged, not knowing what to say to that. Just then Randy Blevins, a boy in their class, came running over holding Kara's apple. "Yo, girls, quit throwing food!" he yelled. Randy liked to yell. He yelled at recess, he yelled on the school bus, and he even yelled out the answers in class.

Kara blinked at him in surprise. "Hey,

how did you get my apple?" she demanded. "Give it here."

She grabbed it back. Randy made a monster face and then ran off with a yell.

"You know the best thing about slumber parties?" Kara said with a frown as she wiped off the apple on her napkin. "No boys allowed!"

"Good thing we're having the party at Taylor's house instead of yours." Jo smiled at Kara. "Otherwise, your brothers would probably try to crash it."

Taylor gasped. "That's a great idea!"

"What?" Kara sounded confused. "Having my stinky brothers crash our sleepover? That sounds like a terrible idea to me."

"No, silly." Taylor rolled her eyes. "The great idea is having the next sleepover at your house. Or Em's. Or Jo's."

"The *next* sleepover?" Jo said.

"Sure!" Taylor tapped her fingers on the

lunch table, looking more excited than ever. "This could be just the beginning. Maybe we could have sleepovers every weekend from now on!"

Kara gasped, dropping her apple again. This time it rolled across the table and bumped into Jo's sandwich. "That's the best idea ever!" she cried, clapping her hands. "Taylor, you're a genius!"

"I know." Taylor grinned. "I can't help it."

Jo looked thoughtful. "We could turn it into a club," she suggested. "Sort of like the bridge club my parents belong to."

"Bridge club?" Kara said. "What do they do—go tour bridges or something?"

Jo giggled. "No, silly," she said. "Bridge is the name of a card game. My parents get together with their friends once a month to play cards and eat dinner."

"Oh." Taylor looked confused now too. "So do you want us to play bridge at our party?"

"I don't know how to play bridge!" Kara complained.

"No, wait!" Jo shook her head. "Listen for a second, okay? I'm trying to tell you. My parents have a bridge club—and we should have a slumber party club!"

"Oh!" Taylor and Kara cried at once.

"A—a slumber party club?" Emily repeated, even more nervous than before.

She was already worried about whether her parents would let her go to *one* sleep-over. Now her friends wanted to form a whole club?

"It's perfect!" Taylor cried. "We could be the Sleepover Friends."

"No—the Sleepover Squad." Kara smiled. "That means the same thing, but it sounds better. Right, Em?"

Emily smiled weakly. She got the best grades of any of her friends in English class. "Sure," she said. "That sounds good."

She couldn't believe this was happening. The first day of the last week of school had started out great, but now it seemed to be getting worse and worse. What if she asked her parents if she could go to Taylor's slumber party and they said no? What if her best friends were all in the Sleepover Squad without her? They would all be having fun together every weekend, and she would be all alone, sitting in her dark room without even a night-light to keep her company. . . .

Suddenly, Emily felt tears welling up in her eyes. She did her best to stop them by swallowing hard and staring down at her lunch.

But it was no use. Right there at the table she burst into tears.

# ✳ 3 ✳

## Emily's Problem

Kara gasped. "Em, what's wrong?" she cried.

Jo put her arm around Emily's shoulders. "Why are you crying?"

"Did you bite your tongue or something?" Taylor asked. "I hate when I do that. Sometimes it happens when I try to talk and eat at the same time."

Emily shook her head, still staring down at her lunch. Her tears hadn't even stopped yet, but she was already embarrassed about

starting to cry right there in the cafeteria.
She hoped the kids at the other tables
hadn't noticed.

"I—I'm okay," she said with a gulp and
sniffle. She squeezed her eyes shut until
she could feel the tears stop flowing. Then
she opened her eyes again and wiped them
with her napkin.

She looked up at her friends. They were all staring at her with concern.

"Em, what is it?" Jo spoke up for all of them. "You can tell us."

Emily took a deep breath, wishing she wasn't so quick to cry whenever she felt upset or anxious. She knew that Kara and Jo would never cry over something so silly. And Taylor hardly ever cried at all. She hadn't even cried when she'd sprained her ankle in the middle of her big soccer tournament last year.

"It's stupid," Emily said, so quietly that the others had to lean forward to hear her. "But Taylor's party sounds like so much fun, and I'm not sure I'll be able to go!"

"What?" Kara exclaimed. "You have to go! It'll be no fun without all of us there."

Jo was frowning. "Wait, I think I see the problem," she said to Emily. "It's your parents, right? You think they might not let you go?"

Emily nodded. She was afraid if she said anything, she might start crying again.

"Come on, that's silly, Emmers," Taylor declared. "They've let you come to lots of parties at my house before."

"But not slumber parties," Jo told her.

Kara bit her lip, looking worried. "I get it," she said. "Em's parents are awesome and nice and everything. But they can be a little, um . . ." She paused, glancing over at Jo.

"Old-fashioned," Jo finished for her. "At least about some things."

Emily nodded. "I'm afraid this might be one of those things," she said. "What if they say no?"

"What if they say yes?" Taylor said quickly. "You won't know until you ask them, right?"

"Taylor's right," Jo agreed. "We don't even know if this is going to be a problem yet. You can go home and ask them today, and then we'll know—one way or the other."

Kara clasped her hands together, almost knocking over her juice box. "I hope they say yes!" she exclaimed. "The Sleepover Squad wouldn't be the same without you, Em!"

"Don't think that way," Taylor told Kara. "Like Jo said, they haven't said no yet. So maybe they'll say yes, and everything will be fine."

"I hope so," Emily said. But inside, she wasn't so sure. "I guess all I can do is ask, right?"

"Hi, Emily-Memily," Mr. McDougal said with a smile as Emily climbed into the car. "How was school today?"

"Fine." Emily smiled back, then quickly turned around to pull out her seat belt. She was afraid if she said anything else to her father, she would spill out her news about the sleepover. She didn't want to do that—not yet. It would be better to wait until she could talk to both of her parents together.

She had to bite her lip all the way home to keep from telling. It took only about fifteen minutes to drive from Oak Tree Elementary to the McDougals' green-shuttered old farmhouse on a quiet country lane outside of town. But that day it seemed to take forever. Luckily, Emily's father was in a silly mood. He told jokes and sang along with the radio as he drove. That kept him busy enough not to notice that Emily was being extra quiet.

Finally, they turned in past the McDougal Organic Nursery sign by the mailbox. The car bounced down the long gravel driveway between two rows of tall maple trees. "Last stop! All ashore that's going ashore!" Mr. McDougal sang out.

Emily got out of the car. It was a warm, sunny day, and she could see her mother out in the large vegetable garden at the side of the house. "Let's go talk to Mom for a second," she told her father.

"Are you sure?" Mr. McDougal patted his stomach. "I could use a snack. How about if I make us some cinnamon toast?"

"Um, maybe in a few minutes," Emily said. She was so nervous by now that she knew she couldn't possibly eat anything— not even her father's cinnamon toast. "I really want to talk to you and Mom about something."

"Oh!" Her father looked surprised, but he nodded. "Okay, then. Let's go."

They walked over to where Mrs. McDougal was hard at work weeding a lettuce bed. She looked up at them, squinting even under her wide-brimmed straw hat. Then she brushed the dirt off her knees and stood up.

"Hello, you two," she said. "How was school?"

"Miraculous," Mr. McDougal said. "All my tenth graders passed their pop quiz! But never mind that—it seems Emily has something she wants to say to us."

"Oh?" Mrs. McDougal squinted at Emily. "What is it, sweetheart?"

Emily's mouth felt dry. This was it: She was about to find out whether her last day of school—and maybe the rest of the summer, if not her whole life—would be great or terrible.

"Um, okay," she said, shuffling her feet in the dirt. "See, Taylor had a great idea. You know how she's always having parties, right? And they're always lots of fun, and you always let me go? . . . Well, anyway, she had a new idea for a party. It's to celebrate the last day of school. And her parents said it was okay for her to have a sleepover instead of a regular party this time. It would be just the four of us—me, Taylor, Jo, and Kara. We would stay at

Taylor's and play games and stuff just like a regular party, only this time we would bring our sleeping bags and stay over. . . ."

She was talking as fast as she could. She didn't want to give her parents a chance to say no before they heard her out. But finally, she ran out of breath and had to stop.

"So that's what I wanted to talk to you about," she finished. "Can I go? Please?"

Her parents glanced at each other. Emily's heart sank as she saw her mother frown slightly and shake her head. Her father was pursing his lips the way he always did when he was worried about something.

"I'm sorry, Emily," Mrs. McDougal said after a moment of silence. "I don't think so. Not until you're a little older."

# ✳ 4 ✳

## It's Not Fair!

Emily could hardly believe her ears. "Why not?" she cried.

Her father sighed. "As your mother said, it's just too soon, Emily," he said. "Maybe in a year or so we can discuss it again."

"But Taylor's party isn't in a year or so," Emily said. "It's this Friday! Don't you realize how important this is? If I don't get to go—"

She couldn't go on. From the way her parents were staring at her, she knew her arguments wouldn't change their minds. It was just too unfair. She burst into tears and took off toward the house.

Flinging open the mudroom door, she raced inside and almost tripped over her cat, Mi-Mo, who was sleeping on the rag rug just inside. Mumbling an apology to the startled cat, she continued through the room, up the creaky wooden back staircase, and down the hall to her room. Slamming the door behind her, she flung herself onto the handmade quilt covering her bed.

She grabbed her favorite doll, Annabelle. "It's not fair," she mumbled into Annabelle's yarn hair. "It's just not fair!"

She had been worried all day that her parents might say no. But she still could hardly believe that they'd really done it. None of her friends' parents treated them like that, acting as if they weren't old enough to do anything. Emily figured she might as well plug her night-light back in and stay a baby forever. After all, that was how her parents would always see her.

She sobbed into Annabelle's hair for a while longer. Then, all cried out, she sat up and looked around. The afternoon sunlight was pouring in through her windows, making splashes of brightness on the color-ful hooked rug on her floor. Standing up, she walked over to the window and looked out. She had a good view of the vegetable garden from there. Mrs. McDougal was still out there weeding, while Emily's father pushed a wheelbarrow toward the compost bins at the edge of the woods.

Emily hurried to her bedroom door and opened it a crack. Mi-Mo was standing outside, swishing his tail. When he saw her, he let out an annoyed meow.

"Sorry, Mi-Mo," she whispered. "Come on in."

She let the cat into her room and then tip-toed out into the hallway, making a beeline for the cordless phone on the little table near the top of the front staircase. Grabbing the handset, she scooted back to her room and closed the door again. Normally, she wasn't supposed to use the phone without asking first. But that day she didn't feel like following her parents' rules.

She sat down next to Mi-Mo, who had just jumped up onto her bed. Then she dialed Kara's number. After two rings someone on the other end picked up.

"Who is it?" a loud male voice barked, making Emily jump.

"Um, hello?" she said. "This is Emily. Is Kara home?"

"Kara who?" the voice demanded gruffly. For a second Emily was afraid she'd dialed the wrong number. Then she heard giggles and snorting in the background.

"Eddie? Chip?" she guessed uncertainly. Kara's two older brothers sounded almost alike on the phone.

There was a sudden burst of muffled yelling in the background. For a second there was no other sound. Then Kara's familiar voice came on the line, sounding a little breathless.

"Sorry about that, Em," she said. "My brothers are idiots. But never mind that—what's up? Did you ask them?"

Emily sighed. "I asked them," she said glumly. "They said no. Just like I was afraid of."

"What?" Kara shrieked so loudly that Emily had to move the phone away from her ear. "You're kidding! I can't believe they said no. Are you sure?"

"I'm sure. They think I'm too young for a sleepover."

"How can they say that?" Kara sounded outraged. "You're practically the most mature and responsible person in the whole second grade. Are they crazy?"

Emily sighed again. She could tell that Kara was trying to make her feel better. But instead, she was feeling worse.

"I'd better get off the phone before my parents come inside," Emily said. "Can you call the others and tell them?"

"Sure. And don't worry, Em—we'll figure out something to do about this!"

"Okay." Emily didn't think there was anything her friends could do that would help. But she didn't tell Kara that. "See you in school tomorrow."

She and Kara said good-bye and hung up. Emily returned the phone to its spot in the hall, then closed herself in her room again. She usually loved hanging out in her room. She had picked out the colors herself—pink and yellow—and helped her mother paint the walls. She had her dolls, two shelves full of toy horses, and dozens and dozens of books crammed into the bookcase her father had made out in his workshop. But that day none of it seemed very interesting.

Mi-Mo was sitting with his front legs tucked under his chest, purring loudly. Emily sat down beside him and stroked his glossy fur. Even that didn't make her feel much better.

Half an hour later she heard her mother calling her downstairs to dinner. Emily groaned and pushed herself off the bed.

"Guess I'd better go down, Mi-Mo," she told her cat, feeling grumpy at the thought of facing her parents again. "I wish I didn't have to, though."

She stomped down the steps and into the kitchen. Her father was standing at the stove stirring something, while her mother set the table with the family's cheerful blue and white plates.

"Can you grab the silverware, Em?" Mrs. McDougal said.

Emily frowned. "Do I have a choice?" she muttered under her breath.

Her mother glanced over at her. "What was that, Emily?"

"Never mind." Emily trudged over to the cabinet and grabbed a handful of forks and spoons, letting them clank together as loudly as possible. She tossed a fork and spoon beside each of the three plates on the table, not bothering to straighten them.

She expected her parents to scold her about that. Instead, she saw them exchange a long, serious look.

"All right, people," her father said a moment later. "I think the vegetables are ready. Let's eat!"

Emily ate as quickly as she could. Her stomach felt kind of funny, and she didn't have much of an appetite. But she knew her parents wouldn't let her be excused until she'd eaten something. So she forced down several spoonfuls of peas and carrots and a whole piece of chicken.

"May I be excused?" she asked as soon as she had gulped down the last of her glass of milk. "Please."

Her parents exchanged another glance. Mrs. McDougal's face wore a slight frown, and Mr. McDougal looked somber.

But once again, neither of them said anything about Emily's unusual behavior.

"Yes, you're excused," Mrs. McDougal said.

"Thanks," Emily muttered sullenly. Pushing back her chair, she ran back upstairs.

# ✳ 5 ✳

## Jo's Plan

"Okay," Taylor said. "We need a plan."

The four friends were huddled around Emily's desk in Ms. Byrd's homeroom. As promised, Kara had called the others the previous afternoon to tell them what Emily's parents had said. Emily had filled them all in on the rest of the details when she'd first arrived at school that morning. Now they were all trying to figure out what to do about it.

✳ 46 ✳

"What kind of plan?" Emily asked hopelessly. "You guys know my parents. They hardly ever change their minds about stuff."

"Hey, they just agreed to let you turn off your night-light, right?" Kara pointed out. "Maybe they'll see the light about this, too." She grinned. "Get it? See the *light*? Like night-*light*?"

Jo rolled her eyes. "Hardy har har," she said. "Maybe you should do your stand-up comedy routine at the sleepover, Kara."

Emily bit her lip and glanced around the room, which was filling up with her classmates. She was afraid she was about to embarrass herself by starting to cry again.

"Yeah," she said. "And you guys can tell me all about it the next day, since I'll have to miss it."

"Don't worry, Emmers," Taylor said, reaching over to give Emily a hug. "That's definitely not going to happen. If you can't come, the sleepover is off. We'll do a picnic or something instead. But I'm not ready to give up yet!"

"Taylor's right," Kara said as Jo nodded. "It wouldn't be any fun without you."

Emily was glad the others didn't want to have the slumber party without her. But that made her feel even worse about the whole situation. Her parents weren't just ruining things for her—they were ruining them for her best friends, too!

"Okay, so all we need is a good plan, right?" Kara said, tipping her chair back against the desk behind her. "So who has a good idea?"

"Maybe we should all go over and talk to Em's parents," Taylor suggested, rubbing her hands together. "We can just keep telling them all the reasons we need Emmers there until they have no choice but to give in."

"I have a better idea," Kara said. "Emily could go on a hunger strike! You're so skinny already, Em—if you swore you wouldn't eat again until your parents changed their minds, they'd have to give in. Oh! Or how about this—the silent treatment. Don't talk to them until they say you can come to the party."

Emily was pretty sure neither of those things was likely to work. "Maybe I'd be better off running away from home and coming to live with you," she told Kara, only half joking. "Your parents would never notice another kid around the place."

Taylor laughed. "Now you're thinking!"

"I have an idea."

Jo's voice was quiet. But all three of the others stopped talking and turned to listen. Emily realized that Jo hadn't said anything for a few minutes and guessed that she'd been busy thinking. That made her heart jump with a tiny spark of hope. Jo always came up with the best plans.

"What is it, J?" Taylor asked eagerly. "What's your idea?"

Before Jo could answer, Randy Blevins came racing into the room. He was yelling, as usual. His friend Max Wolfe was yelling too. They skidded across the floor, their

sneakers squeaking. Both of them crashed into Marie Torelli's desk, making her scream. Her backpack fell off the desk, and her papers scattered everywhere.

"Uh-oh!" Max yelled.

Randy hooted with laughter. "Marie made a mess!" he shouted gleefully. "Messy Marie!"

Max and two or three of the other boys in the room started chanting "Messy Marie! Messy Marie!" over and over again. Marie and her best friend, Tammy Tandrich, scowled at the boys and started picking up the papers.

Kara wrinkled her nose as she watched. "Boys," she declared with distaste. "Why do they always have to act so immature?"

"Never mind them." Taylor turned back to stare at Jo. "We have more important things to worry about than stupid boys. Now come on, Jojo—tell us your plan!"

Jo shrugged. "Okay, but it's not really the kind of plan you guys were talking about," she said. "I was just thinking about how Emily told us she was in a bad mood after her parents said no, stomping around and everything."

"I still can hardly believe that part," Kara broke in with a giggle. "Em's never in a bad mood!"

"I guess I was last night," Emily admitted, feeling a little bit guilty about the way she'd acted. "I was just so mad about being treated like a baby—I couldn't help it."

"But see, that's what I'm trying to say." Jo turned to gaze at Emily. "I think the best way to change your parents' minds is to apologize for acting that way."

"What?" Taylor exclaimed. "Why should she apologize? They're the ones treating her like a kindergartner!"

"No kidding!" Kara agreed quickly. "*They* should apologize to *her*!"

"I know, I know." Jo still sounded calm, even though Taylor and Kara were both scowling at her. "But think about it, you guys. After she apologizes, they'll definitely listen if she explains about the slumber party in a more grown-up way."

Emily shook her head, not really sure what Jo meant. "But why?" she said. "They already said no when I tried that before. That's why I was mad in the first place, remember?"

"Okay, but didn't you say you barely had a chance to discuss it before you started crying?" Jo said.

Emily glanced around, hoping nobody else had heard what Jo had said. Luckily, Randy and Max were roughhousing in the back of the room, and most of the kids in the class were back there watching them.

"You don't have to tell the whole world what a crybaby I am," Emily told Jo with a slight frown. "Anyway, this is probably a waste of time. My parents think I'm still a baby, and nothing will change their minds."

Jo shrugged. "But see, that's just the problem. If you act like a baby, they'll keep treating you like one. But if you act more like a grown-up, maybe they'll notice that you *are* growing up."

"Hey!" Taylor said. "Don't be so mean, Jo. Em's not a baby."

"Yeah." Emily could feel tears welling up, and she swallowed hard to stop them. It was bad enough to know that her parents thought she was a baby. If her best friends started to think the same thing, she wasn't sure she could stand it.

Jo put a hand on Emily's arm. "I'm not trying to be mean, Emily," she said. "But think about it. What's the only way your parents might change their minds about letting you go to the slumber party?"

Emily thought about that. "If they think I really am grown up enough to sleep away from home?"

"Right!" Jo said. "And the best way to show them that is *acting* grown up enough. Get it?"

Taylor and Kara exchanged a glance. They both looked doubtful and a little confused.

But Emily realized that Jo was right. Her parents weren't going to change their minds because of some silly hunger strike or give in to Taylor's arguments no matter how long she talked.

No, Jo's plan was the only one that just might work . . . *if* Emily could pull it off.

## ✻ 6 ✻

### Trying Again

E mily's stomach fluttered nervously as she walked out of school that afternoon with her friends. Could she do it? Was she really grown up enough to make Jo's plan work? Or were her parents right—was she still too young to sleep away from home?

"On the ride home, think about all the stuff we helped you come up with," Jo suggested. "You can sort of practice it in your head. Then talk to both your parents together."

"Okay," Emily said. "Thanks, you guys."

"Are you sure you don't want us to come over and help?" Taylor asked.

Emily shook her head. "I think I need to do this by myself."

Her friends waved good-bye. Jo headed toward her bus, while Taylor and Kara, who both walked to school, headed in the other direction. Emily walked to the area in front of the school where parents could pick up their kids. As always, Mr. Purcell, one of the fourth-grade teachers, was there monitoring the pickups, and Emily waved hello to him.

Normally, Emily's father was already waiting for her when she got out. But today there was no sign of the family's old green and brown station wagon. She sat down on the curb to wait.

A girl from a different second-grade class named Wendy Wing walked over to her.

"Hi, Emily," Wendy said. "Looks like your dad is late, huh?"

"Yeah," Emily said. "Maybe he gave one of his students a detention."

Wendy wrinkled her nose. "Is that when they have to stay after school for being bad? I'm glad we don't have detentions yet. Did you know it might rain tomorrow?"

Emily smiled. Wendy always talked like that. She jumped from one subject to another without even pausing for breath.

"I didn't know that," Emily said.

"I like rain," Wendy said, kicking at the curb. "Hey, Emily, I heard Taylor Kent is having a slumber party. Is that true?"

Emily gulped. "You heard that?"

"Everyone is talking about it," Wendy said. "Guess what? I got an A on my spelling quiz."

"That's nice." Emily wasn't really listening to Wendy anymore. She was too worried about what she had just said. If everyone knew about Taylor's party, everyone would also know if it got canceled. And they would probably find out why, too. Everyone would know that Emily was the baby who wasn't allowed to sleep away from home.

She couldn't let that happen. Right then and there, she decided something: If she couldn't go to the party, she would tell her friends that they should go ahead and have it anyway. Even if they had to do it without her.

That decision made her feel sad . . . but also a little bit more mature. And it reminded her that she'd better follow Jo's advice. On the ride home with her father, she would think hard and plan out exactly what to say. Her friends had already given her lots of ideas, so all she had to do was practice so she wouldn't forget anything. It had to be perfect.

"Excuse me, Wendy," Emily said. "I

think I see my dad's car coming."

She stood up as the station wagon pulled in. But when it stopped by the curb, she got a big surprise. Her father was driving, as usual, but her mother was sitting in the front seat beside him!

Emily gulped. It looked as if she wouldn't have time to plan what to say after all.

She took a deep breath as she walked to the car. All she could do was try her best.

"Hello, Emily," her mother said as Emily slid into the backseat. "How was your day?"

"Fine," Emily replied, feeling nervous. "Um . . . Mommy? Daddy? I want to say something."

"Yes? What is it?" her father asked as he drove the car away from the school.

"I'm sorry about the way I acted yesterday," Emily blurted out. She could feel her face turning almost as red as Kara's, and she was afraid she might start crying again.

But she took a few more deep breaths to hold back her tears. After all, mature almost–third graders didn't cry every time they were nervous or didn't get their way.

"Well, thank you for the apology, Emily." Her mother sounded surprised but pleased.

"That's not all," Emily said. "Um, I have something else I want to say. Will you listen all the way through before you say anything? Please?"

In the front seat her parents exchanged a glance and a nod. "Of course," her father said. "Go ahead. Let's hear it."

"It's about Taylor's sleepover." Emily spoke as calmly and carefully as she could. She wanted to sound just as logical and thoughtful as Jo would in her place. "I know you already said I couldn't go. But I hope you'll think about it again. See, I really think I'm old enough and mature enough to sleep away from home. For one thing, you already decided I was old enough to sleep without my night-light. That means I'm growing up. And I think this party is a good way to show that. I can give you all the details about the party, like that it's at Taylor's house, and it starts at five in the afternoon on Friday. I even already planned out what I would need to bring—my nightgown, my toothbrush, a pillow, and a sleeping bag. Taylor already said we can use her toothpaste and wash-cloths."

Emily paused for breath. She looked at her parents. Her father's eyes were on the road as he drove. But her mother was looking back at her from the front seat, her face thoughtful.

"Is that all?" Mrs. McDougal asked.

"Not quite," Emily said. "I just want to say that if you say no, I'm not going to act like a brat. I promise. And I don't blame you if you say no just because of how I acted yesterday." She smiled hopefully. "But I hope you'll say yes."

Her mother nodded. Then she and Emily's father shared a long look.

Emily held her breath. She had done everything she could. But would it be enough? Would Jo's plan work?

# ✳ 7 ✳

## The Big Decision

That Friday afternoon, Emily sat on a stool in the farmhouse's kitchen and watched her father pull a pan out of the oven. He was wearing an apron with a picture of an artichoke on it, along with a pair of oven mitts. He closed the oven door with his knee and then turned around to face Emily.

"Ta-da!" he said, sliding the pan onto a trivet on the counter. He grabbed a platter out of the cupboard beside the stove and set

it nearby. Then he turned over the pan and shook it, which made a dozen cupcakes tumble onto the platter. "Looks like the cupcakes came out perfectly!" he announced.

"That's nice. They smell good." Emily sneaked a peek at the clock on the wall over the refrigerator. It was three minutes after five. Were her friends already at

Taylor's house for the slumber party?

Her father looked over just in time to catch what she was doing. "Don't worry," he said with a smile. "You won't be late. That clock is fifteen minutes fast, remember?"

"Oh yeah, I forgot." Emily grinned at him. She still could hardly believe her speech in the car the other day had worked. Her parents had said she could go to the sleepover!

Just then her mother hurried into the kitchen carrying a basket filled with strawberries. "I just picked these," she told Emily, handing her the basket. "I thought you could take them to the party."

"Thanks, Mommy!" Emily said, grabbing a berry and popping it into her mouth. "My friends will love these."

"You're welcome." Her mother smiled at her. "Now, are you sure you packed everything you'll need tonight?"

"I think so." Emily glanced at the suitcase, pillow, and rolled-up sleeping bag stacked neatly beside the back door. "I have my nightgown, my toothbrush, my slippers, a hairbrush, and some clean clothes to wear tomorrow. Oh, and I also brought Annabelle."

Her father chuckled. "I'm sure Annabelle will enjoy the party too."

"I know she will." Emily was so excited that she shivered. "Thanks again for letting me go, you guys."

"You're welcome," her mother said again. "But you should thank yourself, too. Your father and I were very impressed by your mature apology and explanation in the car on Tuesday."

Mr. McDougal nodded, licking some cupcake crumbs off his fingers. "That's what changed our minds," he added. "You really are growing up into a mature young lady, Emily. Sometimes we forget that."

Her mother stepped forward and gave her a hug. "Yes. But no matter how mature you get, you'll still always be my baby."

Emily hugged her back with the arm not holding the strawberries. For once, she didn't mind at all being called a baby.

Meanwhile, her father was packing up the cupcakes into a large tin. "We're always going to make decisions we think are right for you, Emily," he said. "But we're also always going to be willing to listen to what you have to say if you don't agree with those decisions."

"That's right," her mother agreed. "All you have to do is talk to us, sweetheart."

"I know. I'll remember." Emily smiled at them. She had never been happier to be a part of her little family. Her parents might be a bit old-fashioned, but they were also the best parents in the world.

Of course, that didn't mean she wanted to stay there in the kitchen with them any longer than necessary—at least not today. She had a slumber party to go to. And she couldn't wait!

"Here we are," Emily's father announced, pulling to the curb in front of Taylor's house.

The Kents lived in a big stone house in one of the nicest neighborhoods in town. Huge, leafy trees lined both sides of the street. The trees' gnarled roots made bumps in the white paved sidewalks, and their branches cast shade over the neatly tended front yards.

Emily's heart felt like it was beating twice as fast as usual. She went over to Taylor's house all the time. But today was different.

"Thanks for driving me here," she said.

"No problem. If I'd stayed home, your mother would have made me help her transplant eggplants." Her father winked and grinned to show he was joking around.

"Come on, I'll walk you to the door."

Soon they were standing on the Kents' broad front porch. Emily set down her sleeping bag. She barely had to knock before the door flew open.

"You're here!" Taylor cried. "Welcome to the slumber party! Hi, Mr. M."

"Hi yourself, Taylor," Emily's father

said. He held out the tin he was holding. "Emily and I made cupcakes for the party. We thought you girls could have fun decorating them before you eat them."

"Yum!" Taylor took the tin. "Thanks!"

Just then Taylor's mother appeared behind her. Mrs. Kent usually wore business suits for her job as a financial consultant. But today she was dressed in jeans and a T-shirt.

"Hello there, Emily," Mrs. Kent said. "Hi, Arthur."

"How are you doing, Trenyce?" Emily's father replied. "Are you sure you're up to dealing with this gaggle of girls all night?"

Mrs. Kent laughed. "I think we can manage. Come on in!"

Emily's father helped her carry in her things. Then he got ready to leave.

"Have a nice time, Emily-Memily," he said as he bent down to give her a hug.

While he was hugging her, he whispered in her ear, "Just call us if you get too homesick and want us to come get you. Even if it's the middle of the night."

"Okay." Emily was glad to hear him say that. But she was pretty sure she wouldn't need to call. "Bye, Daddy. See you in the morning."

After he left, Taylor and Emily carried Emily's stuff upstairs to Taylor's bedroom. Taylor dropped Emily's sleeping bag on her fluffy cream-colored rug. Taylor's room was bigger and fancier than Emily's. The Kents had hired a professional decorator to pick out the furniture, carpet, and curtains. The decorator had also chosen the cream and gold wallpaper. But now the wallpaper was almost completely covered by Taylor's sports and music posters. The posters made the room feel a lot friendlier.

"Just throw your suitcase anywhere,"

Taylor told Emily. "We'll set up our sleeping area later."

"So when are Kara and Jo coming?" Emily asked. "I was afraid I'd be the last one to get here."

Taylor opened her mouth to answer. But right at that moment the sound of the doorbell rang through the house. Taylor grinned. "Sounds like they're here now."

The two girls ran back downstairs just in time to see the Kents' housekeeper, Gloria, open the front door. Kara and Jo were standing together in the doorway.

"Yay! Now everyone is here!" Taylor said.

"Hi, Gloria," Kara said politely. Then she rushed inside, tossing aside her duffel bag. "We're here!" she cried. "So let the slumber party begin!"

# ✳ 8 ✳

## Kara Takes the Cake

"Okay, first things first," Taylor announced. "Everybody change into their pajamas!"

Emily blinked in surprise. She had just helped Kara and Jo carry their things upstairs.

Jo wrinkled her nose. "But it's only five fifteen in the afternoon," she said.

"No, she's right!" Kara exclaimed, bouncing up and down on the edge of Taylor's bed. "It's a slumber party. We have to wear pj's!"

"How do you know what to do at a slumber party?" Jo asked. "You've never been to one before!"

But Kara was already digging through her duffel bag. Taylor ran over to her dresser and pulled out a set of frog-print pajamas.

Emily grinned at Jo. "I guess we'd better do what they say."

Soon all four of them were dressed in their nightclothes. Taylor was wearing her frog pajamas and a pair of fuzzy, neon green slippers. Emily had put on her favorite nightgown, which had a pretty blue and yellow flower pattern and lace around the collar. Kara was dressed in a flouncy, bright pink nightie with ruffles. And Jo had on a pair of plaid flannel shorts, a baggy T-shirt, and dark blue slippers.

"Okay, *now* this is starting to look like a slumber party," Kara declared. "So what are we going to do first?"

"We could decorate those cupcakes Emmers brought," Taylor said. "Or maybe we should go play in the rec room for a while first."

Jo raised her hand. "I vote for the rec room," she said. "I dare any of you to try to beat me at Ping-Pong."

"Is that a challenge?" Taylor grinned. She loved challenges. "You're on!"

They all ran downstairs. Taylor's father was just coming in the front door, his suit jacket slung over one arm.

"Hi, Dad!" Taylor called, not even slowing down as she raced down the hall toward the basement door.

"Hi, Mr. Kent!" Emily, Jo, and Kara chorused as they followed.

"Hello, girls," Mr. Kent said with a laugh as they ran past him.

For the next hour the four friends played in the basement rec room. There was a Ping-Pong table down there, along with a pool table, a suction dart game, a TV with a video-game console, and lots of books and board games.

Then Mr. and Mrs. Kent called them upstairs for dinner. Normally when the girls came over to Taylor's house, they ate their snacks or lunch in the kitchen. Tonight, however, they got to eat in the dining room. Gloria had gone home for the day, but she'd left a pot of her delicious spaghetti sauce bubbling on the stove. Mrs. Kent served the spaghetti to the girls accompanied by salad and garlic bread.

"Is it time for cupcakes yet?" Kara asked as she finished her second helping of spaghetti. She burped, then giggled. "Oops! Excuse me."

"It's definitely time for cupcakes," Taylor said. "Emily's dad's cupcakes are so good!"

"We can't eat them yet," Jo reminded her. "We need to decorate them first, right?"

Emily nodded. "Dad sent along some frosting and other stuff for us to use." She stood and picked up her plate. "Let's clear the table, and then we can get started."

Mr. Kent came in from the kitchen just in time to hear her. "Never mind that, Miss Emily," he said, taking the plate from her. "My wife and I will clear up tonight. You girls go ahead into the kitchen—she's already setting up your cupcake factory in there."

"Thanks, Dad!" Taylor skipped over and kissed her father on the cheek as he bent to pick up another plate. "You're the coolest!"

Within moments, the four of them were seated at the kitchen table. The cupcakes were in the middle of the table, along with a bowl of white frosting. All around them were dishes containing different ingredients the girls could use to decorate the cupcakes.

"Wow," Jo said, surveying the choices. "I never heard of decorating cupcakes with strawberries before."

"Why not?" Kara popped a strawberry into her mouth. "It'll make them a lot more interesting than the boring old plain cupcakes from the grocery store."

They all got to work. There were a dozen cupcakes, so each girl got to frost and decorate three. Emily made her first one with pink frosting and strawberries. Then for the next one she traded Jo for some of her pale green frosting and decorated the cupcake with mint leaves from her mother's herb garden. For the third one she kept the icing white and covered the top with different-colored mini gumdrops.

"There!" Taylor said, putting one last pineapple slice on top of her third cupcake. "It's perfect."

"Mine, too." Kara picked up one of her cupcakes and stared at it hungrily. "So can I eat it now?"

The other girls laughed. Kara was always hungry.

"Wait!" Jo said as Kara started to peel back the cupcake paper. She jumped out of her seat. "I brought the digital camera I got for my birthday. Let me take a picture of all the cupcakes before we eat them."

"Okay." Taylor set down her cupcake beside the others. "But hurry up—I don't think Kara can wait much longer!"

When Jo returned with her camera, the girls posed with their cupcakes so she could take pictures of them. Then Taylor took more pictures so Jo could be in them too. Finally, when Mrs. Kent came in to see how they were doing, they asked her to take some pictures of all of them.

"Okay, now it's time to do something even more fun than decorating cupcakes," Kara said. "*Eating* them!"

The girls ate until they were stuffed. Each of them finished two cupcakes.

"We can save the others until later," Taylor said. "We'll probably get hungry again, since we're going to stay up all night."

"We are?" Jo looked alarmed.

"Definitely!" Kara said. "That's what you do at sleepovers. You stay awake playing games and telling spooky stories until the break of dawn."

Emily clapped her hands. "That reminds me," she said. "I just read this really spooky story—"

"Wait! Hold that thought, Emmers."

Taylor stood up and grabbed the plate with the leftover cupcakes on it. "Last one upstairs is a rotten egg."

They ran up to her room. "Let's set out our sleeping bags before we start the stories," Kara suggested.

"Already? But it's not even nine o'clock yet," Taylor said. "You're not thinking about going to sleep already, are you?"

"No way," Kara said. "But I might need to wrap my sleeping bag around me if Em's story is too scary."

They all unrolled their sleeping bags, arranging them in a circle in the middle of the floor. Even Taylor had brought in a sleeping bag for herself. "I don't want to be the only one with a bed," she pointed out. "That wouldn't be fair."

Then they settled down for some spooky stories. Emily went first. She read a lot of books, so she knew lots of stories. One of her stories was so scary, it made Kara scream.

Then Kara took a turn. Her stories weren't very spooky. But they were funny. Soon the others were laughing so hard, they couldn't sit up straight.

Emily had no idea how much time was passing as they took turns telling stories and jokes. All she knew was that she was having a wonderful time. She wasn't even homesick!

"Hey," Jo said after a while. "It's almost eleven o'clock." She yawned.

"Quit yawning!" Taylor warned. "We're going to stay up all night, remember? Come on, let's have a cupcake. That will give us energy."

She grabbed her last cupcake. So did Kara and Jo. But Emily just stared at hers and groaned.

"I'm still too full," she said. "I don't think I can eat another one. One of you guys can have it."

But after finishing theirs, the other girls

were too full too—even Kara. Taylor picked up Emily's leftover cupcake and stared at it.

"I have an idea," she said. "The first person to fall asleep gets this cupcake stuck to their forehead."

Kara laughed. "That's a great idea!" she exclaimed. "Now I *know* I won't be the first one to fall asleep."

"Me neither!" Emily and Jo said at the same time.

"Good," Taylor said. "Now come on—who's in the mood for a game of Truth or Dare?"

That woke them all up for a while. But as midnight came and went, all four of them started yawning, even as they talked and goofed around. Emily was sure one of the others would give in and fall asleep first. After all, she was used to staying awake for hours reading by the light of her night-light.

Soon it was past one o'clock in the morning. Then it was almost two. Taylor's greenish gold eyes were drooping. Kara was huddled in her sleeping bag with both hands propping up her head. And Jo could hardly say two words without stopping to yawn.

"What time is it?" Emily asked sleepily as Taylor finished another spooky story. She was so tired, she wasn't even sure what the story had been about.

Jo checked her watch. "It's two twenty-five," she said. Then she yawned.

Emily glanced at the cupcake sitting in the middle of the circle of sleeping bags. Her eyes felt heavy, and her head seemed to be stuffed full of wool. She wasn't sure she could stay awake much longer. She wondered what it would feel like to wake up with a cupcake stuck to her head with sticky frosting.

Just then she heard a sound from the

direction of Kara's sleeping bag. It sounded like . . . a snore!

She looked over. Kara's head had dropped down onto her folded arms. Her eyes were closed. As Emily watched, her mouth opened and another snore came out.

"Hey!" Emily whispered to Jo and Taylor. "Look. Kara's asleep!"

That made Taylor sit up and look more awake. She grinned. "You know what that means," she whispered.

Jo giggled. "It's your house," she whispered to Taylor, shoving the cupcake toward her. "You do it!"

Taylor grabbed the cupcake. Emily wasn't sure whether to feel sorry for Kara or to laugh. As she pictured Kara waking up in the morning with a cupcake on her forehead, she couldn't help giggling.

Taylor crept forward, the cupcake held at the ready. She moved it carefully toward Kara's forehead. . . .

Just then Kara's eyes fluttered open. She rolled over and looked up at Taylor sleepily. Taylor was so surprised that she froze in place, still holding the cupcake.

"Hey, thanks," Kara mumbled. She grabbed the cupcake and stuffed it into her mouth.

Emily and Jo started giggling again. Taylor rolled her eyes. Kara finished the cupcake, then rolled over and closed her eyes again. Almost immediately, she started snoring softly.

Taylor started laughing too. "Oh well," she said. "So much for that plan!"

"Maybe we should all go to sleep now," Jo said groggily. "It's late, we're all tired. And we don't want to end up sick or grouchy tomorrow. Otherwise, our parents might not let us do this again."

"That's true," Emily said.

Even Taylor nodded, though she looked a little disappointed. "I guess you're right, Jojo," she said. "We'll have plenty of chances to stay up late at other parties."

Emily smiled, glad her parents had changed their minds so she didn't have to miss this. She snuggled down into her cozy sleeping bag, fluffing up her favorite pillow. "Long live the Sleepover Squad!" she said.

"Long live the Sleepover Squad!" Taylor and Jo echoed.

Emily wasn't sure if either of them said anything else, because a second later she was sound asleep.

# ❋ 9 ❋

## Long Live the
## Sleepover Squad!

The next morning Emily woke up to the delicious smell of pancakes. For a second she thought she was in her bed at home and wondered why her mattress felt harder than usual. Then she remembered where she really was and smiled. She sat up and yawned. She felt a little tired but happy.

"Good morning," Taylor said. She was sitting up too. "I was just going to wake you guys up. It smells like Mom is making breakfast."

Emily stretched her arms over her head. "It smells great," she said. "And hey, Taylor, this whole party was really fun. I'm glad I got to come."

"Me too," Taylor said. "And now that you've proved you can sleep away from home, I'm sure your parents will say yes next time, too."

Emily nodded. Taylor was probably right. "Maybe they'll even let me host one at my house soon!" she said.

Jo moaned and rubbed her eyes. "Is it morning already?" she asked. Her voice sounded croaky like a frog, which made Taylor and Emily laugh.

"Rise and shine, sleepyhead," Taylor said. Then she leaned over and poked Kara, who was still sleeping. "Hey! Rise and shine."

It took a while to wake up Kara. But finally, all four of them were up. While they got dressed, they talked about the party and started making plans for the next one.

"I was just telling Taylor, my parents might let me have one at our house soon," Emily told Kara and Jo.

"That would be great," Jo said. "Your house is so much fun."

Taylor nodded. "We can play soccer or softball in your backyard and climb trees in the woods."

"Yeah. And Em's dad is a great cook!" Kara agreed. "Maybe he'll barbecue some hot dogs for our dinner."

"I can ask him," Emily promised.

They were all dressed by then, so they headed downstairs for breakfast. Just as they were finishing their pancakes, the doorbell rang. It was Emily's parents, who had arrived to pick her up.

"Good morning, sweetheart," her mother said, bending down to kiss her on the forehead. "Did you have a nice time?"

"The best!" Emily exclaimed. "We played all kinds of games and told stories and—Oh! The cupcakes turned out great," she added, turning toward her father. "We took pictures."

"Yes, they were delicious, Mr. M," Kara said.

That reminded Emily of how Kara had woken up just long enough to eat that last cupcake. She glanced over at Taylor and started to giggle. Taylor giggled too. Then Jo joined in.

Kara looked confused. "What?" she demanded. "What's so funny?"

They all took turns explaining. Before long even Kara was laughing. "That sounds like something I'd do," she admitted.

Then Emily picked up her things, which Mr. Kent had fetched from upstairs. "Bye, you guys," she said. "Happy first official day of summer vacation."

"Happy first official day of summer vacation to you too, Emmers," Taylor said. "Thanks for coming to my sleepover."

Kara and Jo added their good-byes. Then Emily thanked Taylor's parents and followed her own parents out the door. Her father put an arm around her shoulders as they walked toward the car.

"Sounds like the party was a success," he said.

"It was." Emily smiled up at him. "But I missed you guys."

She saw her parents exchange a glance. "Really?" her mother asked, sounding a little worried.

"Yes," Emily said. "I definitely missed you. But not *too* much." She laughed. "I can't wait for the next slumber party!"

# Slumber Party Project:
# Frosting Frenzy

Emily and the others had tons of fun decorating their own cupcakes with unusual toppings. Why not give it a try at your next party?

Start with plain cupcakes (homemade or store-bought, chocolate or vanilla—it doesn't really matter).

Buy or make plain white frosting. You can add food coloring to create different colors (ask an adult to show you how).

Then find anything you can to decorate your cupcakes! You can use normal stuff, like sprinkles or chocolate chips. Or you can go crazy-creative and try some more unusual toppings. Here are a few ideas: fresh berries; mint leaves; dried fruit; mini marshmallows; coconut flakes; walnut chunks; or pieces of candy, like gumdrops or peppermints. Use your imagination! One tip: Stick to the sweet stuff. Cupcakes topped with olives or tuna fish are just gross!

Once your cupcakes are decorated, do as the Sleepover Squad did and savor the moment by taking pictures. Make sure everybody at the party gets to pose with her favorite cupcake. Later on, the photos will remind you not only of your fancy cupcakes, but of the whole sleepover.

Then comes the best part of all: eating your creations! Make sure there are no leftovers . . . or you never know what might happen!

P. J. DENTON

# Sleepover Squad

## #2 Camping Out

Illustrated by Julia Denos

# Sleepover Squad

## #2 Camping Out

# * 1 *

## A Summery Sleepover

"Okay, you guys," Taylor Kent said. "It's time to decide where we're going to have our next sleepover party."

Taylor and her three best friends were spending a sunny midsummer afternoon at the Maple Street Swim Club. They had just spent a couple of hours playing tetherball and Marco Polo. Now they were drying off by lying on their beach towels at the edge of the main pool.

Kara Wyatt groaned and reached up to

squeeze more water out of her thick, wavy red hair. "Do we have to decide now? It's too hot to talk!" she said.

"It's been hot all summer," Taylor teased. "And you still manage to do plenty of talking."

Jo Sanchez laughed. "Good one, Taylor."

Instead of answering them, Kara flopped over from her back to her stomach

and let out another loud groan. She liked to be dramatic that way.

Emily McDougal sat up and reached for her tube of sunscreen. Emily had very fair skin that burned easily. Her parents insisted that she reapply her sunscreen at least every couple of hours.

She squirted white goo out of the tube and started rubbing it on her arms. "I guess

we should talk about it soon," she said.

But she didn't sound very eager. Sitting out in the sun seemed to be making everyone except Taylor feel a little lazy. Taylor almost never felt lazy. Her mother liked to say that she had been born doing jumping jacks and that she hadn't slowed down since.

"We were supposed to have a sleepover every weekend, remember?" Taylor reminded her friends. "That's why we formed the Sleepover Squad. But it's been over a month since the first party at my house."

Emily stopped rubbing in sunscreen for a second and squinted at Taylor. "That's true," she said. "I didn't realize it had been that long."

"It *has* been a while." Jo sat up. She tilted her head to one side, the way she often did while solving problems at the board in math class, then said, "Thirty-three days, to be exact."

Taylor smiled. Jo always liked to be exact. "So what are we waiting for?" Taylor asked. She scraped her big toe across the scratchy pavement at the pool's edge. Then she dipped it into the cool water. "One of you needs to ask your parents if you can have the next party."

"Yeah." Kara yawned. "I would do it, but my older brothers just got home from baseball camp. And they don't leave for soccer camp for two weeks." She wrinkled her nose. "And, of course, my little brothers are home all summer."

Taylor smiled sympathetically at her friend. Kara was always complaining about having four rambunctious brothers. She made them sound like monsters, and it was true that they could be pests some-times. Still, Taylor thought it might be kind of fun to have a bunch of other kids around all the time—even boys. It would be like having her own personal basketball team, right there in the same house.

"Okay, Kara's place is out," she said. "Emmers? What about you? You were talking about maybe having the next sleepover at your house, right?"

Emily nodded and pushed back a strand of her damp, pale blond hair. "I remember," she said, but she sounded distracted. She squirted out another dollop of sunscreen.

Taylor watched her. Emily had already put on sunscreen twice since they'd arrived at the pool. Taylor was glad she didn't have to worry that much about sunscreen—her African-American skin didn't burn as quickly as Emily's very pale skin did. "So did you ask your parents?" she asked Emily.

"Not yet, but I—Oh!" Suddenly, Emily sat up straight, looking excited. The sunscreen tube slipped out of her hand and bounced on the pavement. Jo caught it just before it rolled into the pool.

"What's wrong, Em?" Kara sat up and

stared at her. "Did a mosquito bite you? They've been biting me all day." She scratched at a pink bump on her freckled arm, then at another on her ankle.

Emily smiled. "No, not a mosquito," she said. "But a great idea just bit me!"

It took Taylor a second to figure out what her friend was saying. Sometimes Emily talked like someone from one of the books she was always reading. It could be a little confusing. Taylor always found it easier just to say what you meant straight out.

"You mean you have an idea?" Taylor asked. "Is it about our next slumber party?"

"Yes." Emily's blue eyes sparkled. "I just remembered something. My parents got a new tent last week. I could ask them if we can use it. That way, we could camp out in the backyard for our next sleepover!"

Jo gasped. "That would be so much fun!"

"Definitely!" Kara clapped her hands.

Her freckled cheeks were already pink from being out in the sun all day. But now they went even pinker with excitement. "What an amazing idea! It's the perfect summer sleepover plan!"

"I can ask my dad to cook hot dogs for us on the grill," Emily said. "And being outside in the dark will make our spooky stories even spookier!"

"My mom always talks about going camping," Jo said. "She used to camp out with her sisters and cousins all the time when she was our age. She likes to tell stories about catching fireflies and falling asleep to chirping crickets."

Taylor was glad the others were finally getting excited about the next sleepover. But she wasn't very excited about the camping idea herself. She stared out at the people splashing around in the pool, trying to figure out how to tell her friends that.

"Listen, guys," she said. "Camping could be fun. But it might be too hot to sleep outside."

Emily shrugged. "My house doesn't have air-conditioning," she said. "So we'll be hot either way if the party is at my house."

"Oh." Taylor hadn't thought of that. "Okay. But what if it rains?"

"It's not supposed to rain until next week," Jo said.

Taylor didn't bother to question her. Jo usually knew what she was talking about. "Okay," she said, trying to think of another argument. "But—"

"Hey, Em, do you have a croquet set?" Kara interrupted eagerly. "I've always wanted to learn to play croquet. But our yard isn't big enough. Plus, my brothers would probably just beat one another over the head with the mallets."

Jo giggled. "That sounds like your brothers."

"We have a croquet set," Emily said with a smile. "I'll teach you how to play, Kara."

"Can we fly kites?" Jo asked. "My mom talks about doing that a lot too."

"That sounds like fun," Emily agreed. "When I ask my parents about the campout and the croquet set, I'll ask them if we can get the kites out of the attic."

Taylor opened her mouth to argue against the campout idea. But then she closed it again. She could tell it was no use. Everyone in the Sleepover Squad was excited about their plan of sleeping outside in a tent. Everyone except her.

She bit her lip, not sure what she was going to do. How could she admit the *real* reason she didn't want to camp out?

## 2

## Taylor's Secret

Just then Jo looked at her watch. It was waterproof, so she could wear it even at the pool. "Hey, Taylor," she said. "You told me to tell you when it's almost two fifteen. It's ten minutes after two right now."

"Thanks." Taylor jumped to her feet and picked up her towel. "I've got to go. I have soccer practice today."

Kara looked disappointed. "But we just started planning our campout sleepover!" she complained.

"That's okay. You guys can keep planning without me." Taylor smiled, trying to seem normal. She didn't want her friends to guess her secret. Not until she figured out the best way to tell them. And right now she didn't have time — she didn't want to be late for soccer practice.

She said good-bye, grabbed her pool bag, and headed toward the exit. There was no running allowed in the pool area, so Taylor just walked as quickly as she could. The hot cement burned her feet, but she didn't put on her flip-flops until she reached the big metal gates at the entrance. Then she paused long enough to slip them on.

She spotted a familiar bright blue car as soon as she stepped through the gates. The car belonged to the Kents' housekeeper, Gloria. Both of Taylor's parents had busy jobs, so Gloria was the one who drove Taylor around during the day. Luckily, Taylor could walk to the swim club from her house, so Gloria didn't have to drive her there. Taylor was also allowed to walk to Kara's house or to the ice-cream parlor as long as she told Gloria where she was going and called when she got there. But her soccer league met on a field at the high school, which was a couple of miles away at the edge of town.

Taylor stepped out onto the gravel parking lot. She had to walk carefully so no gravel would get between her toes.

"Put your towel on the seat," Gloria said when Taylor opened the car's back door. "You're soaking wet."

Taylor didn't think that was true. In fact, her hair and bathing suit were almost dry. But she did as Gloria said and spread her towel on the backseat before she got in. It was always easier to do as Gloria said.

Gloria started the car. Then she looked at Taylor in the rearview mirror. "You all right, *chica*?" she asked. "You look a little down."

Taylor usually made a joke when Gloria called her *chica*. She knew that *chica* was just a Spanish word for "girl." But she always pretended she thought Gloria was calling her a chicken.

Today, however, Taylor wasn't in a joking mood. She hated keeping secrets from her friends. Now, suddenly, she found herself with a big one. And it definitely wasn't the kind that would be easy to share.

"I'm okay," she said. "Hey, Gloria, I was just wondering something. Are you afraid of anything?"

Gloria stopped the car at a stop sign. Then she glanced back at Taylor again. "Me, afraid?" she said. "Why do you ask?"

"No reason," Taylor said quickly. She wasn't ready to tell anyone what was worrying her. "I was just curious."

She already felt a little bit silly for asking. Gloria wasn't the type of person to be afraid of anything. She was always telling stories about all the crazy things she and her brother had done while growing up in Puerto Rico.

"Oh." Gloria shrugged. "Well, if you must know, I do have a terrible fear of heights. Once my brother convinced me to climb a very tall tree. When I reached the top branches, I was too terrified to climb down again. Our papa had to come out and rescue me." She laughed. "He teases me about it to this day!"

"Really?" Taylor grinned. It was funny to imagine Gloria, with her carefully pressed clothes and neat black and gray bun, clinging to the branches of a tree. "So you were really afraid?"

"I was really afraid," Gloria said. "I also don't like looking out windows in tall buildings or driving over large bridges. I know it's silly, but those things always make me feel dizzy and anxious."

"Wow." Somehow, hearing that even someone as sensible as Gloria had silly fears made Taylor feel a tiny bit better about her own secret.

"I'll tell you something else that frightens me," Gloria said. "It's that you won't have your soccer clothes on by the time we get to the field."

"Oops!" Taylor realized they were almost there. She grabbed the bag of clothes on the car floor and pulled on her shorts and T-shirt over her swimsuit. She was still lacing up her cleats when Gloria turned the car into the high school parking lot.

The playing fields were swarming with kids. At least three summer league teams, including Taylor's, were practicing that day. When she got out of the car, she looked for the bright green T-shirts that matched the one she was wearing. The shirts said MCDOUGAL ORGANIC WARRIORS on them. Taylor's team was named after Emily's mother's plant and vegetable business, McDougal Organic Nursery. The nursery was the team's sponsor, which meant Mrs. McDougal helped pay for the uniforms and equipment.

Taylor said good-bye to Gloria. Then she jogged across the fields toward the other kids in green shirts. Several of her teammates saw her coming and waved or shouted out her name.

"Yo, Kent!" a boy named Curtis Cohen called. "It's about time you showed up."

"Zip your lip, Cohen," Taylor yelled back with a grin. "No matter what time I show up, I still play better than you!"

Another teammate, Essie Anderson, laughed and gave Taylor a high five. "You tell him, Taylor," she said. "Curtis couldn't score a goal even if the net was ten miles wide."

Taylor giggled. She knew Essie was just kidding around. Curtis was one of the best players on their team. In their last game he'd scored more goals than anyone except Taylor.

Curtis ran over and gave Essie a playful shove. "Oh yeah?" he said. "The only thing around here that's ten miles wide is your mouth!"

Just then the assistant coach, a college student named Chloe, walked toward them. "Get stretching, people," she called out. "We'll be starting in a few minutes."

Taylor dropped to the grass and started

doing the stretching exercises the coaches had taught them. Essie sat down beside her.

"Were you at the pool today?" Essie asked between stretches. "I can see your bathing suit straps under your shirt."

"Yeah, I just came from there," Taylor said as she leaned forward to touch her toes. "My friends and I were . . ."

She forgot what she was saying mid-sentence as she felt somebody grab the back of her shirt. A second later something small and wriggly tickled her back.

"Hey!" Essie cried. "Very funny, Curtis!"

"Check it out!" a boy standing nearby shouted gleefully. "Curtis put a spider down Taylor's back!"

"Ooh, watch out, Curtis!" another teammate cried. "She's going to pound you for that one."

"She'll probably stick that spider up his nose!" someone called out with a laugh.

But Taylor hardly heard what any of them were saying. She leaped to her feet, shaking her arms and yelling. "Get it off me!" she shrieked. "Get it off me!"

She could feel the spider wriggling down her back. The sensation made her feel panicky. She jumped up and down and spun around in circles. The more she moved, the more she seemed to feel the

spider's hairy little legs scrabbling around on her skin. It felt as if there were spiders crawling all over her!

"Chill out, Taylor," Essie said. "It's just a spider. Hold still and I'll—"

"Don't tell me to chill out!" Taylor yelled. *Just get it off!*

Chloe hurried over. "Hold still," she ordered sharply.

The assistant coach's voice stopped Taylor's jumping for a second. Chloe grabbed Taylor by the shoulder, spun her around, and tugged at the back of her shirt.

"There it is!" Essie cried, pointing. "It just fell out."

Taylor leaped forward. Then she glanced back over her shoulder and saw a small black creature scurrying off through the grass. Her whole body went limp with relief.

She looked around and found almost the

whole team gathered around. Her team-mates were all staring at her in surprise.

"Yo, check it out, guys," Curtis said, his eyes wide with amazement. "Tough Taylor Kent is afraid of bugs!"

# ☀ 3 ☀

## Never Surrender!

Taylor didn't embarrass easily. But she was embarrassed now. She couldn't believe the whole soccer field had just heard her terrible secret. It was true: Ever since she could remember, she'd been scared of having spiders or other creepy-crawly types of bugs touch her. Most people never would have guessed it. After all, Taylor loved playing sports and being outdoors. But even the idea of tiny little legs crawling on her gave her the creeps.

"Shut up, Curtis," she muttered, hanging her head and staring at her own feet. "You're so immature."

Chloe clapped her hands. "All right, people," she said. "I see Coach Summers heading this way. Let's take your places. . . ." She started calling out which positions she wanted everyone to take.

Taylor was glad. She wanted to stop thinking about what had just happened. She jogged toward her position as soon as Chloe called her name.

Essie quickly fell into step beside her. "Don't worry, Taylor," she said. "It's no big deal if you don't like spiders. I freak out if I even *see* a snake. And my uncle is afraid of mice."

"Yeah, okay." Taylor didn't feel like talking about it anymore. "We'd better get in position now."

A moment later the coach arrived and practice started. Curtis made spider fingers at Taylor the first few times he passed close to her. But nobody else said anything about what had happened. By the time they started doing shooting drills, even Curtis seemed to forget all about it.

Still, Taylor couldn't stop thinking about it. She missed two easy shots in a row because she was so distracted.

"Focus, Kent!" the coach barked at her.

"Sorry," Taylor called out.

She was annoyed with herself. It was bad enough to be afraid of something so dumb. But it was even worse to let it ruin her game.

As she walked back to the end of the line, she realized there was one good thing about what had happened. Now there was no reason not to tell her friends why she didn't want to camp out. She might as well admit she was terrified at the thought of sleeping on the ground, where all kinds of spiders and other bugs could crawl on her. Now that her entire soccer team knew, the news would be all over town before long.

Taylor made a face. How could a thought like that make her feel better and worse at the same time?

As soon as she got home, Taylor headed for the phone in the front sitting room. Gloria was busy in the kitchen at the back of the house, and neither of Taylor's parents was home from work yet. That was good. Taylor didn't want anything to interrupt her. Once she made up her mind to do something, she liked to do it right away.

She dialed Emily's number first. Someone answered on the second ring.

"Good afternoon," a crisp voice said. "McDougal Organic Nursery. How may I help you?"

"Hi, Mrs. M," Taylor said, recognizing

Emily's mother's voice. "This is Taylor. Is Emily there?"

"Hi, Taylor. I'm sorry, she's not home right now. She and her father just left for the grocery store to get supplies for your party."

Taylor was surprised. "She asked you about the sleepover already?" she asked.

Mrs. McDougal chuckled. "Yes," she said. "She was so excited, she couldn't wait. It's going to be tomorrow night—if you can make it then?"

Taylor thought about saying she couldn't come the next night. But she didn't think about it for long. She hated lying.

"Yes," she said instead. "I think I can make it then. I just need to check with my parents to be sure."

She said good-bye and hung up. Then she stared at the phone and chewed on her lower lip. Was it already too late to change her friends' minds?

"No way," she whispered to herself. "All I have to do is explain why we need to move the party inside. . . ."

She picked up the phone again. This time she dialed Kara's number. All she got was a busy signal. She hung up and tried again. Same thing.

"Rats," she said. "Stupid brothers."

Kara's house had only one phone line. Her brothers were always tying it up by spending hours playing goofy computer games online. They always got in trouble when Kara's parents caught them. But they always ended up doing it again.

With a sigh, Kara punched in Jo's number. Jo was the most sensible of them all, anyway. If Taylor could make her understand, Jo could help her explain it to the others.

Jo's mother answered the phone. "Oh, hello, honey," Mrs. Sanchez said when she heard it was Taylor. "Jo just got picked up for her tennis lesson. Is this about your campout tomorrow night? Jo's so excited about it, and no wonder! Some of my favorite memories involve camping out. . . . But never mind. Shall I have her call you when she gets home?"

"Um, no, that's okay," Taylor said. "It's nothing important. Thanks anyway."

After Taylor hung up, she flopped onto the antique sofa in front of the fireplace. She wasn't usually the type of person who wasted a lot of time sitting around worrying. But today she couldn't help it. Her friends were all superexcited about the campout idea. How could Taylor ruin their fun just because she was a wimp when it came to bugs?

Just then the front door swung open. "Hello, hello! Anybody home?" Taylor's father cried, striding in with his suit jacket slung over one shoulder.

"Dad?" Taylor sat up, surprised.

Normally, her father didn't arrive home from his law office until just before dinnertime. "What are you doing home so early?"

Mr. Kent turned and spotted her. He had a big grin on his face as he walked into the sitting room.

"I decided to give myself the rest of the afternoon off," he said. He dropped his jacket on the arm of the sofa and reached over to give Taylor's head a rub. "I'm celebrating—I just won that big case I've been working on all summer."

"Really? That's cool." Despite her worries, Taylor smiled. It was nice to see her dad in such a cheerful mood.

"It's more than cool." Her father grinned. "Everyone and their brother expected me to lose this case, and lose big. But I guess I showed them!" He winked. "Just goes to prove my motto: Never surrender!"

Taylor giggled. Her father's good mood was catching. She already felt a little bit

better than she had a few minutes ago.
"Never surrender!" she said, pumping her
fist. "Congratulations, Dad."

Her father hurried off toward the kitchen
to share his news with Gloria. Taylor stayed
where she was. She was thinking about
what he had just said.

Maybe she was looking at this campout situation all wrong. Maybe her dad's motto could work for her problem, too. Why should Taylor give in to her own fears? Why should she let the thought of a few creepy crawlies spoil everybody's fun, including her own?

Suddenly, she was glad she hadn't reached any of her friends on the phone. Because she had just decided *not* to tell them about her fear . . . at least not until *after* the campout the next night. That way, by the time she told them the truth, it wouldn't matter anymore. By then she would have overcome her silly fear.

"Never surrender!" she whispered to herself.

# 4

## The Big Day

Taylor had a nervous knot in her stomach when she woke up the next morning. For a second she couldn't remember why. She lay there sleepily, staring up at her ceiling. Did she have a big game today? Was it already the first day of school? Or . . .

Suddenly, she remembered: Today was the day of the campout. That made Taylor wake up in a hurry.

"Never surrender," she whispered to

herself again. Then she sat up and swung her feet over the edge of her bed.

If she was going to do this, she was going to do it full speed ahead. That was just the way she was. So for the next few hours she barely stopped moving. She did everything she could think of to get ready for the sleepover. She took everything out of her dresser drawers and closets so she could decide which clothes and pajamas to pack. She vacuumed the inside and outside of her suitcase. She packed and unpacked her things twice. She wrote down ideas for games and activities for that night. She called her friends to see how their preparations were going.

"I'm glad you're so excited about the campout," Emily said when Taylor called her for the third time. "At first I wasn't sure you were."

Taylor didn't know what to say to that. Luckily, Emily's mother called her just then, and she had to get off the phone.

Finally, it was time to leave for Emily's house. Kara's mother had offered to pick up Taylor and Jo and drive them to the party. Taylor waited for her outside on the front porch with her suitcase, sleeping bag, and pillow. She spotted the Wyatts' minivan as soon as it turned onto her street.

Kara was riding in the seat right behind her mother. She waved through the open window. Taylor grabbed her stuff and jogged down the front walk.

"Sorry, Taylor!" Kara called. "We're stuck riding with the bratty boys. They insisted on coming along."

"Kara!" Mrs. Wyatt warned. "Don't talk about your brothers that way."

Kara rolled her eyes when her mother wasn't looking. Taylor grinned and slid open the van's back door.

"Hi there, Carrottop Twins," she said.

That was what she always called Mark and Todd Wyatt. They were six years old and looked almost exactly alike, from their tousled red hair to their scuffed sneakers. The only way to tell them apart was by the pattern of freckles on their faces.

"Hi, Taylor," Todd said as Taylor took a seat next to Kara, right in front of the two boys. "We decided to come to your sleepover too."

"Fat chance!" Kara cried, turning around to glare at them.

Mrs. Wyatt glanced at the kids over her shoulder. "Don't tease your sister, boys," she said with a smile. "You know this slumber party is for girls only."

"Girls stink!" Mark said, sticking out his tongue at Kara.

"Boys stink worse!" Kara replied.

Mrs. Wyatt sighed. "Can't you kids *try* to get along for at least ten minutes?"

But Kara and her brothers argued the

rest of the way to Jo's house. The Sanchez family lived in a nice subdivision at the edge of town. Their house was on a cul-de-sac with four other houses. When Mrs. Wyatt drove in, Jo was standing in her front yard watching her teenage neighbors play basketball.

Soon she was squeezed in beside Taylor in the backseat while Kara apologized for her brothers' presence. "It's okay," Jo said with a grin. "Actually, it's lucky there's no more room in the van. Otherwise, I think my mother would have invited herself along to the campout. She's even more excited about it than I am!"

Mrs. Wyatt smiled at Jo in the rearview mirror. "Does your mother enjoy camping?" she asked. "That's nice. I wouldn't have guessed that about her."

It gave Taylor a weird feeling whenever she remembered that all their parents didn't know one another that well. How could that be the case, when the four of them were such good friends?

But she didn't think about that for long. It took less than ten minutes to drive from Jo's house to Emily's. That meant it wouldn't be long until the camp-out started. In just a few hours they

would all be sleeping in a tent outside. Or *trying* to sleep, in Taylor's case.

*Never surrender,* she reminded herself silently.

When they reached Emily's house, Mr. McDougal came out with Emily to help the other girls unload their things from the back of the van. Taylor stacked her sleeping bag on top of her suitcase on the front lawn.

"Well, hello, fellows," Mr. McDougal said cheerfully as Kara's brothers hopped out of the van. "I didn't realize you two were in there."

Kara spun around and scowled at the twins. "Get back in the car!" she said. "You're not supposed to get out."

"It's okay, Kara," Emily said. She sounded a little bit worried. Emily didn't like it when people fought. She always tried to smooth things over if she could. "We don't mind if they run around for a few minutes. Right, Daddy?"

"Right." Mr. McDougal ruffled Todd's hair as the little boy darted past him. "There's plenty of room to run here."

That was true. Emily's yard was bigger than Taylor's, Kara's, and Jo's put together. There was a wide front lawn and an enormous vegetable garden off to the right side of the house. That was all Taylor could see from the driveway. But she had been there often enough to know that there was a fruit orchard behind the garden. Next to that was a large, grassy backyard. It was almost as big as the sports fields at the high school. A forest came right up to the yard on two sides, and on the far side of the orchard was a neighboring farmer's hay field.

"Thanks, Arthur," Mrs. Wyatt said gratefully to Emily's father. "It would be nice for them to get some energy out."

"Maybe they'll run away and never come back," Kara said, sounding grumpy.

She scowled as she watched the boys run around.

Taylor made a scary monster face as Mark ran toward her. "Aaargh!" she growled playfully.

Both twins screamed and raced off in the other direction. Taylor laughed. No matter what Kara said, her brothers could be fun sometimes.

"Come on," Emily said to her friends. "We can come get your stuff in a little while. I want to show you the tent!"

"Cool!" Jo said eagerly.

"I'll be right there," Taylor said. "First I need to catch the twins and throw them in the creek. Aaargh!" She chased after the boys for a few steps. They screeched with laughter and kept running across the yard.

Meanwhile, Emily headed for the front door. "Hey," Kara called, sounding surprised. "Where are you going, Em? Did you set up the tent inside the house?"

Mr. McDougal was still chatting with Mrs. Wyatt. But he looked over when he heard Kara's comment.

"We didn't set up the tent yet," he told her. "If you girls are going to sleep in it, you also have to help me set it up."

"Cool!" Jo said again. "That sounds like fun."

Taylor gulped and turned away from the twins. Every time someone mentioned the tent, she got more nervous.

She followed her friends inside. Emily's house was even older than hers. It had creaky wooden floors, two staircases, and lots of interesting nooks and crannies. There were plants everywhere. Pictures of plants hung on the walls. Books about plants loaded the bookshelves in every room. Real plants in colorful pots sat on all the windowsills.

The girls hurried through the kitchen

and out to the mudroom. That was a sunny room at the back of the house between the kitchen and the back porch. It contained the washer and dryer, a wall of hooks for hanging up coats, and food and water dishes for Emily's cat, Mi-Mo.

The tent was lying in the middle of the floor. At least Taylor guessed it was the tent. It looked more like a big, messy pile of dark blue canvas and metal poles.

"Is that it?" Kara wrinkled her nose. She didn't look impressed.

Emily nodded. "Don't worry, it looks a lot better when it's up. We can start putting it together as soon as Daddy gets here. First we'll need to screw together these poles, and . . . oops!"

She dropped the pole she was holding. Then she giggled.

"What?" Jo asked.

Emily pointed. "That spider startled me," she said. "When I picked up the pole,

it started to crawl onto my hand."

Taylor shuddered. The campout hadn't even started yet, and the first spider had already appeared!

She watched while Emily grabbed a baseball cap hanging on one of the coat hooks. Using the hat's stiff brim, she carefully picked up the spider and carried it to the back door. Jo opened the door for her, and Emily gently dumped the spider outside.

Taylor shuddered again as the door closed. Normally, it wouldn't bother her to *see* a spider as long as it didn't *touch* her. But today was different. Today all she could think about was that in a few hours she would be sleeping outside, where lots of spiders might crawl on her. The thought made her skin crawl.

Could she really do this?

# ✳ 5 ✳

## Fun and Games

The others didn't notice Taylor's reaction. Emily's parents had just walked into the mudroom.

"Ready to get started on the tent, girls?" Mr. McDougal asked. "I hope we got all the pieces out of the attic. Otherwise, you might have to take turns staying awake to hold up the roof!"

Kara and Emily giggled. Jo looked doubtful.

"I don't think that would work," Jo said.

"All the poles probably have to be connected together. If even one is missing, it couldn't stand up at all. Not even with someone holding it."

That made Taylor laugh a little. "Don't worry, Jojo," she said. "I think Mr. M was only kidding around."

"Oh." Jo looked slightly sheepish. "Yeah, I knew that."

Mrs. McDougal grabbed the stack of poles. "I've got these," she said. "You four can help Emily's dad carry the fabric outside."

Taylor hung back as her friends crowded forward to grab the edges of the canvas. The skin on the back of her hands felt itchy as she thought about that spider. What if the spider had a friend still hiding in the folds of the tent? What if there was a whole nest of baby spiders in there, just waiting to swarm out over her arms?

"Can you get that corner, Taylor?" Emily said.

Taylor blinked and stepped forward. "Um . . . okay." She grabbed the fabric, but she used only the ends of her fingers to hold it.

Mrs. McDougal had already dropped the poles outside. She returned to hold open the back door. It was hard for the others to walk together and carry the tent through the narrow opening. But Jo started calling out "left, right, left, right," and soon they had the tent out in the backyard.

Taylor dropped her corner as soon as she could. She backed away and looked down at her hands. No spiders.

She felt kind of stupid for being so nervous. She wasn't supposed to be scared of anything! But she couldn't seem to stop thinking about bugs and spiders.

The others were already sorting out the poles and screwing them together. Taylor walked around and poked at tent parts with the toe of her sneaker. She was trying to look like she was helping without having to touch the tent very much.

Luckily, the others were having too much fun to notice. Taylor was relieved. Maybe she could pull this off after all!

Before long the tent was up. It had a pointy top and a zippered flap for a door. Thick ropes held down the corners to keep it from blowing in the breeze. They had set it up in a nice, open spot on one side of the back lawn, halfway between the wooden picnic table and the edge of the woods. When they were all quiet, they could hear the burble and splash of the little stream that tumbled along a few yards inside the tree line.

"This is awesome!" Jo said, her brown eyes shining as she looked around.

Kara nodded, clapping her hands. "Let's go check out the inside now," she said.

"We can tell stories or something."

"Have fun, girls," Mr. McDougal said. "Let me know when you get hungry, and I'll fire up the grill."

"Thanks, Daddy," Emily said.

As Mr. and Mrs. McDougal walked away, Emily, Kara, and Jo crowded through the door flap. Taylor took a deep breath and followed them. She had to duck her head to fit through.

Inside the tent it was dim and shadowy. The thick, dark-colored canvas kept out most of the sun's light.

"Shouldn't we bring some flashlights or something?" Taylor asked. Her eyes darted around to the dark corners. Were there creepy crawlies hiding back there? It would be awfully easy for spiders or other bugs to crawl in through the openings in the canvas. . . .

"We'll get some lanterns from the house later," Emily said. She sat down cross-legged on the canvas floor. "It's light enough for now, though."

Taylor wasn't so sure. She wasn't afraid of the dark. But being inside the dimly lit tent was making her nervous. She watched as Jo and Kara sat down too.

"Hey!" she said, backing toward the flap. "Are you guys nuts? We shouldn't waste a perfect summer day inside—even if it's inside a tent! I thought we were going to play croquet and fly kites and stuff. And I brought a soccer ball in case we want to play keep-away or something."

"But sitting in here is fun too," Kara said. "Maybe we should hang out for a while."

"No way." Taylor shook her head. "We have all night to sit around in here."

Emily giggled. "You guys should know by now that it's impossible to get Taylor to sit still," she told Kara and Jo.

Taylor was glad nobody had guessed the real reason she wanted to leave the tent. "That's right," she said. "If you don't come outside, I'll go get my soccer ball and start kicking it around in here."

Jo stood up. "Come on, you guys," she said. "I think she means it." She led the way out of the tent.

Once she was out in the fresh air, Taylor immediately felt much better. As long as she was busy running around and doing things, she wouldn't have time to think about scary bugs.

"So what do you want to do first?" she asked the others. She was in the mood for soccer, as usual. But she didn't say so. Now that they were outside, she didn't really care what they did.

"Croquet," Kara said. "Em, you promised to teach me to play."

Emily went to get the croquet set, and the girls played for a while. Emily taught Kara the rules, but Kara wasn't very good. She kept hitting her own foot with her mallet. Then she would say "ow" and start giggling. Taylor and Emily both played a little better than Kara, but Jo won the first three games in a row.

"Maybe all my tennis lessons helped make me good at croquet, too," Jo said. "And I didn't even know it!"

Taylor grinned. "I guess so," she said. "I'll have to practice more if I want to win next time." Taylor was the best of all her friends at sports. Usually the only thing Jo could beat her at was tennis. Now she would have to add croquet to the list.

After one more game of croquet—Jo won again—they switched to Freeze Tag. By the time the last person was "frozen" for the third time, everyone was getting hungry and thirsty.

Kara collapsed to the ground. "I'm dying of thirst," she moaned. "I can't play anymore."

"Okay, let's go inside," Emily said. "Mom squeezed a whole pitcher of lemonade earlier."

Taylor licked her lips. Mrs. McDougal's homemade lemonade was delicious. "Let's go!" she said.

Soon they were back outside, each of them holding a tall, icy glass of lemonade. They carried them over to the picnic table. Taylor checked the wooden seat carefully before she sat down. No spiders.

Mr. McDougal came outside and hurried over to the grill, which was nearby. He lifted the cover.

"I'll get this started," he told them. "The hot dogs should be ready in fifteen or twenty minutes."

"Great." Kara patted her stomach. "After all that running around, I'm starved!"

Emily giggled. "You're always starved," she teased.

"That's true. But right now *I'm* starved too," Jo said. "My mom always says camping made her hungrier than just about anything else."

"It's more fun than just about anything else too!" Kara said. "Hey, maybe *all* our summer sleepovers should be campouts from now on."

Taylor's heart sank when she heard that. But she didn't say anything.

In fact, she didn't say anything for the next ten minutes. She sat there sipping her lemonade and sneaking looks at the tent standing nearby. How many spiders were crawling around in there right that minute?

Finally, Jo noticed how quiet she was being. "Earth to Taylor," she joked. "What's got you distracted now?"

The others also turned to look at her. Taylor thought about just telling them all the truth. As her mother liked to say, that was always the easiest answer.

Then she thought about what her father liked to say: Never surrender. That made her wonder if admitting her fear to her friends might be like giving up. She knew her friends would offer to move the sleepover inside if she told them what was bothering her. But how could she overcome her fear if she didn't face it?

"Nothing," she said, deciding to stick with her plan. She would tell them the truth in the morning—not before. "Except that I'm starving to death!" She turned in her seat to look at Emily's father, who was poking at the hot dogs sizzling on the grill. "Hey, Mr. M, when are those dogs going to be hot?"

# ✷ 6 ✷

## Wasting Time

By the time the girls finished eating their dinner of grilled hot dogs, lemonade, and a delicious salad of fresh greens picked from Mrs. McDougal's garden, the sun was starting to go down. Kara sat back and burped.

"Excuse me," she said with a chuckle.

"There's no excuse for you," Taylor joked. Even though she was worried about her problem, it was still fun being with her friends.

"Come on, let's take our dishes inside," Emily said, standing up. "Then we can change into our pajamas and come back out."

The girls gathered up their paper plates, napkins, and forks. When they got inside, they found that Mr. and Mrs. McDougal had brought their suitcases and sleeping bags into the mudroom.

"Grab your pajamas. We can change up in my room," Emily suggested.

Taylor loved Emily's room. It was filled with books, toy horses, and pretty handmade quilts and rugs, which made it the perfect room for Emily. Her cat, Mi-Mo, was sleeping on the bed. When the girls came in, he woke up and sat up. Then he started washing his foot with his pink tongue.

While the others started changing, Taylor wandered around, looking at the titles of the books on the bookshelves. But she wasn't really paying attention to the books. Instead, she was thinking good thoughts to try to pump herself up for the sleepover. It was the same thing she did before every big soccer game. Before a soccer game she usually thought things like *I can help my team win this game* and *Go for the goal.* This time she was thinking, *Camping out is great* and *Spiders are no big deal.* Her good thoughts almost always worked before a soccer game. But they weren't working too well tonight. She still felt nervous.

Kara looked up from pulling on her pink nightie. "Hurry up, Taylor," she said. "We want to get back out there."

"Yeah," Jo said, holding up her toothbrush. "And we still have to brush our teeth."

Taylor realized the others were all changed already. "Okay," she said. "You guys can go ahead to the bathroom if you want. I'll be right there."

The others hurried out of the room, talking about how they should arrange their sleeping bags in the tent. Taylor watched them go. Then she picked up her favorite frog-print pajamas, which she'd dropped on Emily's bed. Mi-Mo stopped licking his foot and watched her.

"I'm just being silly, aren't I, Mi-Mo?" Taylor said to the cat. "Bugs and spiders are nothing to be afraid of. I probably stomp on dozens of them by accident every time I play soccer."

Mi-Mo answered by licking his paw again. Taylor sighed. The later it got, the more she worried about spiders crawling on her while she slept. She was annoyed with herself for being so scared. But she couldn't seem to do anything about it.

She changed into her pajamas as slowly as she could. As she was putting on her slippers, Emily returned.

"Are you ready yet?" she asked. "I left the toothpaste cap off for you."

"Thanks." Taylor smiled at her friend.

Once again, she was tempted to tell the truth. If anyone would understand, Emily would. After all, she was afraid of all sorts of things—big dogs, speaking in front of the class, crossing busy streets, and more. And she didn't seem to mind if other people knew it.

But Taylor wasn't like that. She hated

being afraid. That was why she was determined to get over her fear of bugs.

Kara appeared behind Emily in the doorway. "Hurry up!" she cried impatiently. "It's time to get this campout started for real!"

"Okay, okay," Taylor said. "Just let me brush my teeth and I'll be ready. I'll meet you guys downstairs."

"No way," Kara said. "You're too distractible. If we leave you in the bathroom by yourself, you'll probably forget what you're doing and start taking a bubble bath or something."

Taylor's friends were always teasing her about being distractible. Taylor didn't mind; she *was* distractible. There were always so many different interesting things to look at, do, or think about that it was impossible to focus on just one.

But tonight was different. Tonight Taylor was focused on only one thing: surviving the campout.

All three of her friends waited in the bathroom doorway while Taylor brushed her teeth. Then they dragged her downstairs. Mrs. McDougal was transplanting tiny plant seedlings at the kitchen table while Mr. McDougal washed dishes nearby. The tiny, old-fashioned black-and-white TV set on the counter was tuned to the local PBS station.

Seeing the TV gave Taylor a sudden idea. "Oh, I love this show," she said. "Maybe we should stay inside and watch it for a while."

Mrs. McDougal turned and stared at her in surprise. "You love this show?" she said. "I had no idea you were an opera fan, Taylor."

"She's not, Mommy," Emily said with a laugh. "She's just kidding around. Right, Taylor?"

"Um, right." Taylor looked around the kitchen for some other ideas. "Hey, you guys—remember how much fun it was decorating those cupcakes at our last party? Maybe we should do that again tonight. We could help Mr. M bake the cupcakes, and then—"

Kara didn't let her finish. "Forget it. This is a campout party, not a cupcake-making party!" She grabbed Taylor's arm and dragged her through the kitchen and into the mudroom.

When they got there, Taylor spied Mi-Mo's food dish. "Uh-oh, Emmers," she said. "Looks like your kitty is almost out of food." She pointed to the dish. "Maybe we'd better help you feed him."

Emily looked at the dish. "It's almost half full," she said. "I usually only have to fill it in the morning. Don't worry, he'll be fine."

Kara was still holding on to Taylor's left arm. Now Jo grabbed the right one, laughing.

"Come on, Miss Distractible," she said.
"We're supposed to be having a campout,
remember? Camp*out*. That means we need
to go *out*side."

Taylor couldn't think of any other ways
to delay. So she picked up her sleeping bag

and pillow and went out the back door with the others.

It was almost dark by now. Stars were twinkling in the sky overhead, and a slight breeze cooled the warm summer air. Crickets were already starting to chirp, along with the little tree frogs that lived near the stream in the woods.

Kara stopped and took a deep breath. "Aah, this is more like it," she said happily. "I can't wait to get this campout started!"

Emily had grabbed a pair of battery-powered lanterns from the mudroom. She turned them on and led the way into the tent. The lanterns made the inside almost as bright as a room in the house.

Taylor joined in with the others to unroll sleeping bags and fluff pillows. She was getting more and more nervous, though she did her best to hide it. How was she ever going to fall asleep out here?

Then she had an idea. It was much

better than the opera-watching idea or the cat-feeding idea. In fact, it was so simple and so brilliant that she couldn't believe she hadn't thought of it before.

She wasn't really afraid of bugs when she was awake—well, not unless obnoxious Curtis Cohen put one down her shirt, anyway. And she was pretty sure none of her best friends would ever do something like that.

So there was just one solution. She wouldn't go to sleep tonight!

Right away she felt much better about the whole campout. She turned and grinned at her friends. Kara was sitting cross-legged on her sleeping bag. Emily was adjusting one of the lanterns. Jo was flicking a stray leaf off her pillow.

"Okay, guys," Taylor said brightly, clapping her hands. "It's time to have some fun at this party!"

## 7

## Staying Awake

"Okay," Emily said to Taylor. "What do you want to do first?"

Taylor thought for a second. What would help keep them all awake? "I know," she said. "Flashlight Tag!"

"Flashlight Tag?" Kara sounded dubious. "What's that?"

"It's sort of like Freeze Tag," Taylor explained. "Only instead of touching someone to freeze them, you need to catch them with your flashlight beam. It's the perfect game to play in the dark!"

Emily looked nervous as she glanced at the tent doorway. "That sounds a little scary."

"Yeah," Kara said. "It figures Taylor would come up with it. She probably thinks the rest of us will be so scared of the dark that she's sure to win!"

"Very funny," Taylor said as the others laughed. "Now come on. Are we playing or what?"

"I guess we could try it for a while," Jo said. "We all brought flashlights, right?"

Soon they were all outside playing Flashlight Tag. Taylor volunteered to be "it." Each of the other girls turned off her flashlight and sneaked off into the dark.

Taylor closed her eyes and counted to fifty to give them time to scatter. Then she opened her eyes. "Ready or not, here I come!" she called. She switched off her flashlight too.

Then she stood still for a minute, just listening. It felt kind of strange being outside in her pajamas. But it was also kind of fun.

There was some light coming from the house. Everywhere else in the yard was pitch-black. Being out in Emily's yard was much different from being in town, where there was always light from the streetlamps and from cars driving by. It was even darker than Jo's neighborhood, where there was usually plenty of light from the neighboring houses.

Taylor's heart beat a little faster, and she smiled. This was fun!

She heard a rustling sound nearby. It was coming from the direction of the woods. *Aha!* Taylor thought.

She tiptoed toward the sound. She had to move slowly so she wouldn't trip over a rock or a dip in the ground. When she thought she was close enough, she stopped and listened. The rustle came again.

Taylor lifted her flashlight and aimed it. Then she hit the button to turn it on.

"Gotcha!" she cried. Kara was standing there in the beam of light, looking wide-eyed and startled.

"Rats!" Kara said, flicking on her own flashlight. "I wanted to go farther away. But I was afraid I'd wander into the woods and get lost." She shuddered. "Plus, what if there are bears or something in there?"

Taylor rolled her eyes. "There are no bears around here," she said.

"Are you sure?" Kara glanced over her shoulder at the dark trees. Then she wrapped her arms around herself and shuddered. "There could be bears."

"You can ask Jo if you don't believe me," Taylor said with a smile. "Now come on—since I caught you, you get to help me find the others. Then you're it next time."

They kept playing for a while. When it was her turn to hide, Taylor hurried all the way to the orchard. She picked the oldest apple tree there and hid behind its thick, gnarled trunk. The others would never catch her there!

She was still hiding behind the tree when she heard a shriek. It came from closer to the house. She peered out from behind the tree trunk and saw that all three of her friends had their flashlights on.

A few seconds later she heard her friends calling her name. She turned on her own flashlight and jogged toward them.

"What's up?" she called. "Did I win that round?"

"Never mind that." Emily gestured toward Jo, who was sitting on the ground. "Jo hurt herself."

"I'm okay." Jo had one flip-flop off. She

was holding up her toe, staring at it with her flashlight. "I just stubbed my toe, that's all. I guess I tripped on something."

Emily looked worried. "I think it's too dark to play outside any longer," she said. "We'd better go back in the tent."

Taylor's heart sank. She wanted to convince her friends to stay outside. But she didn't want them getting hurt.

Emily was the first one to reach the tent. As she held open the flap for the others, she yawned.

"Uh-oh!" Kara teased. "Are you going to be the first one to fall asleep, Em?"

"You can't be sleepy yet!" Taylor said. "We haven't told spooky stories yet. Or played Truth or Dare. Or even had dessert!"

"Dessert?" Kara licked her lips. "Hmm, that's true. What's for dessert, Em?"

"Ice cream," Emily said, suddenly looking much more awake. "I almost forgot! Daddy bought us a whole gallon of chocolate chip."

Kara was already heading back out of the tent. "So what are we waiting for?"

Twenty minutes later the girls were back in the tent eating their ice cream by the light of the lanterns. When they finished, Taylor suggested playing a game of Truth or Dare. The others agreed, even though Kara was starting to yawn too.

But after a few minutes Taylor noticed something. "Hey!" she said. "You guys are all choosing truth!"

Jo yawned. "I can't help it," she said. "It's easier to answer a truth question. I'm too tired to do any of your crazy dares, Taylor."

"Me too," Emily admitted.

"Me three!" Kara added.

Taylor frowned. All of her friends were lying down on their sleeping bags. If she didn't do something, she was pretty sure it wouldn't be long before all three of them were nodding off to sleep. . . .

# ✳ 8 ✳

## Spooky Stories and
## Scary Dreams

"**O**kay!" Taylor called out, sitting up so suddenly that her foot banged into her ice-cream bowl. She grabbed the bowl and set it beside her pillow for safe-keeping. "Enough Truth or Dare. It's time for spooky stories!"

Emily yawned so widely that her eyes squinched shut. "I don't know if I can think of any right now," she mumbled sleepily. Since she read so many books, Emily was usually the one to start off the storytelling.

"Don't worry, I'll start," Taylor offered. She knew that if she could come up with a really good story, Emily and Kara would be too nervous to fall asleep. Jo was a lot harder to scare, but so far she looked the most awake anyway.

"Go ahead," Jo said. She was lying on her stomach with her head resting on her arms. "We could use a good bedtime story."

Taylor thought for a second. She wanted to make sure her story was *really* scary. Before she started talking, she leaned over and turned down the lanterns. She didn't make it too dark, though. For one thing, that might make her friends even sleepier. For another thing, it might make the spiders think it was safe to come out and start crawling on them.

"This is the tale of a girl named . . . uh, Susie," Taylor began. She made her voice sound as spooky as she could. "One day Susie was going for a walk in the woods when she heard a mysterious sound from just ahead. . . ."

She kept going, making up the story as she went along. Lowering her voice to a raspy whisper, she explained how Susie followed the mysterious sounds until she came to a haunted graveyard. There, she was chased by a gang of terrifying ghosts. They swooped after her as she ran away as fast as she could through the dark forest.

Her friends listened silently for a while. Emily's eyes opened a little wider. She started to look more scared and less sleepy. Kara sat up and hugged her knees to her chest as she listened. Jo didn't look very scared yet, but she was listening too.

". . . and Susie kept running and running, dreading the feeling of ghostly fingers on the back of her neck," Taylor intoned eerily.

Emily shuddered and touched the back of her own neck. Kara glanced nervously into the corners of the tent. Taylor smiled. They both looked pretty scared.

"And then something horrible happened," she went on. "Susie was so busy looking over her shoulder to see how close the ghosts were getting that she didn't pay attention to where she was running. She tripped over a tree root and fell right into a big hole in the ground! At first she was afraid the ghosts would be able to catch her there. But then she realized something even more horrible. . . ." Taylor paused for effect.

"What?" Kara asked breathlessly.

"The hole was very dark," Taylor said. "So dark that she couldn't see anything. But then she heard something—a terrible growl! When the moon came out from behind the clouds, Susie realized she was trapped in a hole with a—um . . ." She paused again, trying to think of something really scary. "A—a horrible, oozing, one-eyed giant squid!"

"Wait a minute," Jo said in her most logical tone. "Squids don't growl. Besides, squids live underwater. How would a giant squid survive in some hole out in the forest? That doesn't make sense."

Taylor frowned. Maybe she should have stuck with a bear or a zombie. "It's *my* story," she said. "I get to decide what makes sense."

Kara giggled. "Maybe it's really a zombie squid. Those can probably live on land. Anyway, that's a pretty good story, Taylor. Much better than the ones my brothers tell when they're trying to scare me."

"I'm not finished yet!" Taylor said. "Anyway, the squid reached out its tentacles . . ."

But it was no use. Kara kept making silly comments about the zombie squid and making fun of the rest of the story, too. Taylor guessed that was what she did when her brothers tried to scare her. And when Kara wasn't joking around, Jo was pointing out all the ways the story couldn't really happen. Before long even Emily didn't look scared anymore.

Taylor did her best to ignore them and keep going. But she noticed that her friends were starting to look sleepy again. She was starting to feel pretty sleepy herself. After a while she couldn't think of anything else to add to her story. There was a moment of silence that stretched on and on. Finally, the silence was broken by the sound of Kara snoring softly.

*Maybe I was worried about nothing,* Taylor told herself drowsily. She leaned back and rested her head on her pillow. *After all, I haven't even seen a spider since we've been out here. . . .*

The thought drifted off into the night air, and she was asleep.

Taylor wasn't sure how long she had been asleep. But suddenly, she felt herself come sharply awake. She knew right away that she was in the tent. But what had woken her?

A second later she felt something touch her face. Something soft and light, like tiny, hairy legs brushing against her forehead.

*"AAAAAAAAAAH!"* she screamed at the top of her lungs.

# ✴ 9 ✴

## Taylor Tells the Truth

"What is it?" Emily cried out, sounding terrified.

There was a moment of commotion as the others woke up. Taylor opened her eyes and sat up quickly, brushing at her own face. The lanterns were still on, and Taylor saw Mi-Mo darting out of the tent with his long, fuzzy tail whipping behind him.

She looked down. Her ice-cream bowl was still beside her pillow where she'd left it, but now the spoon was on the ground.

Feeling foolish, Taylor realized what had happened. That hadn't been a giant spider running its hairy legs over her face. It had been Mi-Mo's tail or whiskers brushing against her as he licked the leftover ice cream out of the bowl.

"Hey, what's the big idea, Taylor?" Kara sounded annoyed. She rubbed the sleep out of her eyes and glared at Taylor. Her red hair was sticking up in tufts on her head. "So we didn't think your story was that scary—that doesn't mean you have to try to scare us like that."

Taylor blinked in surprise. Then she realized that her friends thought she'd screamed on purpose to frighten them.

"But—but I didn't—," she stammered.

"It's okay, Kara," Emily said quickly, trying to smooth things over. "Taylor was just being Taylor. It's no big deal."

"I'm sorry, guys." Taylor felt terrible. "I didn't mean to scare you. I swear."

"Fine." Kara still sounded grumpy. "Does that mean we can go back to sleep now?"

There was the sound of a window sliding open in the house. "Everything all right out there, girls?" Mr. McDougal called.

Emily leaned out the tent's entrance. "We're okay, Daddy," she called back. "Sorry about the noise."

Meanwhile, Jo was peering at Taylor's face. "Hold on," she said to Kara and

Emily. "Taylor looks really upset. What's wrong, T?"

Taylor hesitated for only a second. "Okay," she said. "I guess I should tell you guys the truth." She took a deep breath. "I—I thought a spider was touching me. That's why I screamed."

Kara looked confused. "Huh?" she said. "Is this the start of another story? A giant spider to go with the giant zombie squid?"

"Nothing like that." Taylor shook her head. "See, there's something you guys don't know about me. I—I'm sort of afraid of bugs. At least when they're touching me." She quickly explained her fear.

"Why didn't you tell us?" Kara cried when Taylor had finished.

Emily shook her head, looking amazed. "I can't believe fearless Taylor actually has a fear," she said.

"Yeah." Taylor looked down at her sleeping bag. She was glad she'd finally told her friends the truth. But she also felt embarrassed. "I guess I'm not so tough after all."

Jo scooted closer and put an arm around Taylor's shoulders. "Don't say that," she said. "You're still the toughest person I know."

"Yeah." Kara smiled at her. "And don't worry—we won't tell anyone else. You know you can trust us."

"I know. But that's okay," Taylor said. "My whole soccer team knows now." She told them what had happened at practice the day before.

Emily pushed back her sleeping bag. "I just wish you'd told us sooner," she said. "I never would have wanted to do this campout if I knew you didn't want to. Come on, let's go finish the sleepover inside. My parents won't mind."

"Good idea," Jo said, and Kara nodded.

Taylor thought about it. Sleeping

inside would be a lot easier. . . .

But then she shook her head. "Never surrender," she whispered.

"What did you say?" Kara asked.

Taylor smiled. "I said, we don't have to go inside," she said. "I survived this long out here, didn't I? If I can make it through the rest of the night, maybe I won't be so scared next time."

"Are you sure?" Emily asked, still looking worried.

"Positive," Taylor said firmly.

Her friends traded a glance. They all shrugged.

"Okay," Jo said. "But at least let us help you. We can rearrange our sleeping bags so yours is in the middle. That way, at least the spiders will crawl on us first."

"Ew!" Kara said with a shudder. But she got up and started moving her sleeping bag right along with Jo and Emily.

Taylor was touched. "Thanks, guys," she

said as she watched them circle her with their sleeping bags. "You're the best friends ever."

"We know," Emily said with a smile.

As Taylor drifted off to sleep again a few minutes later, she was feeling better than she'd felt in two days. Why hadn't she told her friends the truth sooner? She still had to face her fear. But this way, she got to do it with her friends on her side.

At least she would know better next time. Because with the whole Sleepover Squad protecting her, she was pretty sure nothing would wake her up before morning.

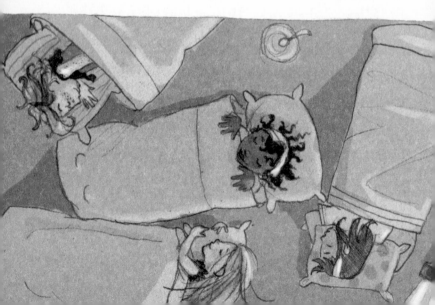

## Slumber Party Project:
## Camping Dos and Don'ts

Do check the weather. Make sure you pack the right type of pajamas for the season, plus anything else you might need, such as sunscreen or bug spray.

Do play games like Freeze Tag or Kick the Can before it gets dark. Go for a nature hike or play ball with the dog. Camping isn't just sleeping in a tent—it's all about having fun outdoors.

Do look up at the stars. See how many constellations you can spot!

Don't use perfume or anything else with a strong scent. Otherwise, you'll be even easier for the mosquitoes to find!

Don't sleep in the same clothes you wore all day.

Don't forget your flashlight. You can use it to make shadow puppets in the dark or to find your way to the restroom . . . or to play Flashlight Tag!

# P. J. DENTON

# Sleepover Squad

## #3 The Trouble with Brothers

Illustrated by Julia Denos

# Sleepover Squad

## #3 The Trouble with Brothers

# ✸ 1 ✸

## Kara's Turn

"I love ice cream!" Kara Wyatt said with a happy sigh. She gazed at the double-chocolate cone in her hand, trying to decide which side to lick first.

Kara was sitting on a bench outside the ice-cream parlor. Two of her best friends, Emily McDougal and Jo Sanchez, were sitting beside her. Their other best friend, Taylor Kent, was hopping back and forth over a crack in the sidewalk. Taylor wasn't very good at sitting still.

"We heard you the first nine times you said that, Kara," Taylor teased. She hopped over the sidewalk crack again. Then she took a big bite from her maple-walnut cone.

Emily licked strawberry ice cream off her lips. "That's okay," she said. "I agreed with her all nine times. And I agree again."

"That means you agreed with her ten times," Jo said. Jo liked to be exact.

Kara took a big slurp of her ice cream. It tasted great, but it made her shiver a little. It was a crisp autumn afternoon, and the air felt cool even though the sun was shining.

A sudden breeze rattled the leaves of the big maple trees lining the street. It also blew a few strands of Kara's springy red hair across her face. The hair almost got into her ice cream, but Kara moved her cone away just in time.

"Brr." Jo was holding back her shoulder-length dark hair with one hand. "Pretty soon it will be too cold to eat ice cream anymore."

"No way!" Kara cried. "It's never too cold to eat ice cream."

"But it *will* be too cold to eat it outside." Taylor wrinkled her nose and looked down at the long brown-skinned legs sticking out of her denim shorts. "And it'll be too cold for wearing shorts. Or for swimming, or soccer, or lots of other stuff. Fall stinks!"

"That's not true! Don't forget all the great stuff about fall," Emily said.

Kara smiled. Emily liked to look on the bright side of everything.

"Like what, Em?" Kara asked.

"Like getting to go back to school," Emily said.

Kara groaned loudly. School definitely wasn't one of her favorite things about fall, or any other time of year. She loved getting to see all her friends every day, and she also loved the chance to get away from her four obnoxious brothers for a while. But other than that, she didn't like much about school.

"It figures Emmers would think of school first," Taylor said with a grin. "After all, her grades are always the best in the class."

Emily blushed. "That's not true." She tugged on a strand of her pale blond hair until it fell over her face. "I got a B minus in gym last year, remember?"

That was Emily. She was shy, and didn't like to brag about anything.

Kara didn't really understand that. If she got almost-straight-As like Emily and Jo did, she would be bragging about it all the time!

"I've got one," Jo said. "In fall the leaves turn pretty colors."

Kara looked around and saw that Jo was right. The big shade trees along Main Street were bright with all the colors of a sunset—orange, red, yellow.

While Kara was looking around at the trees, she spotted Jo's mother walking from the drugstore to the video rental shop next door. Mrs. Sanchez had picked the girls up after school and driven them to the ice-cream parlor. When she finished her shopping, she was going to drive them all home.

Thinking about that reminded Kara of something. "I know another good thing about fall," she said. "Back-to-school shopping! I got lots of good stuff this year."

"Right," Taylor agreed. "And what about Halloween? That's one of the coolest things about fall."

"Ugh," Kara said. "Not when you have four stupid brothers, it isn't. It's their favorite time to try to scare me."

"But what about all that candy?" Jo asked.

Kara took another lick of her ice cream. "Okay, so *that* part of Halloween is pretty cool," she said.

Emily smiled. "See? There are lots of reasons to look forward to fall."

"I've got an idea for another reason," Jo said. "A sleepover!"

"That's an awesome idea," Taylor exclaimed. "We haven't had a sleepover in ages!"

"I call it this time!" Kara cried, jumping up from her seat. She was so excited that she almost dropped her ice-cream cone. "It's my turn to have the sleepover at my house!"

"Cool," Taylor said. "How about doing it this Saturday?"

Jo nodded. "Today is only Tuesday," she said. "That should give us plenty of time to plan. I'll go ask my mom right now if I can go. Hold my ice cream for a second, okay?"

Kara watched as Jo handed her ice-cream cone to Emily and then hurried toward the video store. She wished her mother was there too. She could hardly wait to ask her parents about the party. Kara, Jo, Taylor, and Emily had formed the Sleepover Squad a few months earlier, but they hadn't held a slumber party at Kara's house yet.

"This is going to be great," Kara said. "We can make popcorn, and rent movies, and tell stories till after midnight. . . ."

Just then, Taylor pointed to Kara's arm. "Uh-oh," she said. "Looks like you have a few extra freckles."

Kara looked down. She had been so

busy talking about the sleepover that she'd forgotten to keep eating. A few drops of chocolate ice cream had melted and dripped down onto her arm.

"No problem," she said. She switched her cone to her other hand, then licked the ice-cream drops off her arm. "Now hurry up and eat, everybody. I need to get home and start planning the sleepover!"

"I'm home!" Kara shouted as she burst into her house a few minutes later.

Her second-oldest brother, Eddie, was just coming down the stairs. Eddie was thirteen and thought he was much cooler than Kara.

"Big deal," he said. "Are we supposed to throw a party or something?"

Kara ignored him. She was too excited to let her brother's teasing bother her. She was glad she lived only a few blocks from the ice-cream parlor. That meant Mrs. Sanchez had dropped her off first. And *that* meant she wouldn't have to wait any longer to ask her parents about the sleepover.

She headed straight toward the phone on the little table in the front room. Both her parents worked as engineers, and they usually didn't get home until dinnertime. Up until this year, one of Kara's aunts or older cousins had come over every day to babysit. But now that Chip was fifteen, her parents had decided he was old enough to watch the four younger kids after school.

Kara dialed her mother's office number. "Hi, Mom?" she said when her mother picked up. "It's me. . . ."

She quickly explained about the sleepover. Then she held her breath while she waited for her mother's answer.

"I suppose that would be all right," Mrs. Wyatt said. "I'll call your friends' parents and let them know the party is on."

"Yay!" Kara cheered. "Thanks a million, Mom!"

She said good-bye and hung up. Then she danced across the front room and into the big eat-in kitchen. All four of her brothers were sitting at the table. Six-year-old twins Mark and Todd were reading comic books and eating cheese sticks. Chip was kicking a soccer ball back and forth between his feet. Eddie was drinking a glass of orange juice.

"Hi, Kara," Chip said. "Will you get me a cookie from the cookie jar?"

Normally Kara would have said "Get it yourself." But she was in such a good mood that she smiled at her older brother.

"Sure," she said. "As long as I can get one for myself, too."

"Go for it," Chip said. "There are plenty in there."

Kara spun and twirled her way over to the cookie jar on the counter near the oven. "I hope Mom has time to make more cookies before this weekend," she mumbled to herself. Her mother wasn't as good a cook as Emily's dad or Taylor's housekeeper, but everyone loved her chocolate chip oatmeal cookies.

Kara took the lid off the cookie jar and reached inside. But instead of large squishy-soft cookies, she felt something small and hard. With a frown she pulled out her hand.

"Hey," she said. "What's this?"

In her hand were several hard brown lumps. They looked—and smelled—kind of familiar.

"They're cookies," Todd said with a giggle. "Go ahead and eat one."

Mark was giggling too. "Yeah, it's a new kind Mom bought at the grocery store," he said. "They're delicious!"

Just then the family's dog, a pudgy Labrador retriever named Chester, wandered into the kitchen. As soon as he got near Kara, his nose wriggled and his tail started wagging faster.

That was when Kara figured out what was going on. "These aren't cookies," she exclaimed. "They're some of Chester's dog kibble!"

All four boys burst out laughing. "Rats!" Todd cried. "She figured it out!"

"I thought she was going to eat one!" Mark said.

"Yeah, usually she'll eat anything," Eddie added.

Kara felt her face turning red. She tossed the kibble onto the floor. Chester quickly gobbled it up.

"I'm telling Mom," Kara said. She spun around and headed for the kitchen phone.

"Oh, come on," Chip said with a frown. "Can't you take a joke?"

"You *are* a joke," Kara snapped back. She picked up the phone.

"Not so fast, tattletale," Eddie said before she could dial. "I heard you talking to Mom on the phone just now." He

smirked at the other boys. "She's having her little friends over on Saturday for one of their stupid girly slumber parties."

"Ew!" Todd cried.

But Chip was smiling again. "Really?" he said. "In that case, Kara, you'd better not tattle on us. Otherwise, we might decide to do something just as funny during your stupid party."

Kara gasped. "No way!" she cried,

quickly hanging up the phone. "You can't ruin my sleepover! Swear you won't, and I won't tell Mom about the cookie thing, okay?"

"Hmm." Eddie grinned at Chip. "She sounds kind of nervous, doesn't she?"

Kara gulped. She realized she'd just made a huge mistake.

*I forgot the first rule of dealing with brothers,* she thought. *Never show weakness!*

But it was too late. "She *does* sound nervous," Chip said. He kicked his soccer ball into the corner and leaned back in his chair. "And she should. Because I just had a great idea."

"What?" Mark asked eagerly.

Kara scowled. "What?" she echoed.

Chip crossed his arms over his chest. "You have to do everything we say between now and Saturday," he said. "Every. Single. Thing. Otherwise, we'll ruin your sleepover."

# 2

## A Bad Deal

"Are you crazy?" Kara shrieked, so loudly that Chester ran out of the room with his tail between his legs. "There's no way I'm going to be your stupid servant for the next three days!"

"Three and a half," Eddie corrected.

"Yeah, three and a half," Todd agreed. "Can't you add, Kara?"

Mark laughed loudly. "You'd better not make her do your math homework, Eddie. She got a C in math last year, remember?"

"Good point, squirt," Eddie said. "I'll cross that off the list."

"Don't worry. I'm sure we can think of plenty of interesting things for our new servant to do besides math." Chip grinned. "So, Kara, do we have a deal?"

"Get real!" Kara glared at all four of them. "I'm not doing anything you jerks say. I'm calling Mom right now to tell her about this."

She picked up the phone again.

"Okay." Chip shrugged. "But don't say we didn't warn you."

Kara hesitated. She was so furious with her brothers that all she wanted to do was get them in trouble.

But a little voice in her head was telling her to take a deep breath and think about it. The little voice sounded a lot like Jo. That was probably because it was just the kind of thing Jo would say.

So Kara thought about it. She thought about the time her brothers had put frogs in her lunch box. And the time they'd dyed Chester purple. And the time they'd put toothpaste in Kara's shampoo bottle, and shampoo in her toothpaste tube.

Her brothers didn't let anything stand in their way when they were playing pranks. Not even their parents. Even if Kara tattled, she knew they would find a way to carry out their threat.

She hated feeling so helpless. Usually she wasn't afraid to fight back against whatever her brothers dished out. But this was different. She couldn't let them ruin her sleepover. What if her friends never wanted to come to her house again? It could ruin the whole Sleepover Squad!

When she thought about that, Kara felt like bursting into tears. She wanted to stand up to her brothers, but she couldn't. Not without putting the Sleepover Squad at risk.

That meant she had no choice. She hung up the phone.

"Okay," she said. "I won't call Mom."

"And we have a deal?" Eddie said.

Kara scowled. "It's a deal."

"Good," Chip said. "In that case we can get started right now. I'd like a grape, please. Go get me one."

Kara stomped over to the refrigerator. She yanked open the door and grabbed the bowl of green grapes from the shelf inside.

"Here you go," she said. She dropped the bowl of grapes onto the table.

Eddie reached for the grapes. But Chip stopped him.

"Hold it," he said. "I didn't ask for *grapes*. I asked for *a* grape."

Kara blinked at him. "Huh?"

"I want *one* grape," Chip said. "Not a whole bunch of grapes. Try again."

"Give me a break," Kara muttered. She pulled one grape off the bunch and dropped it onto the table in front of Chip. "There you go. *One* grape. Happy now?"

"Not really." Chip picked up the grape and stared at it. "Those other grapes are in my way."

Without a word Kara grabbed the bowl. She returned it to the refrigerator and shut the door.

When she turned around, she saw Chip popping the grape into his mouth.

"Mmm." He smacked his lips. "That was tasty. Servant, I think I'd like another grape."

Kara glared at him. She could already see where this was going.

She opened the refrigerator and reached inside. She wished she could take the whole bunch of grapes and throw it at her brother's head. Instead, she plucked another grape off the bunch and walked over to the table.

"There you go," she said. "Another grape."

"That looks good," Eddie spoke up. "Servant, I think I'd like a grape too."

Mark and Todd giggled as Kara marched back to the refrigerator. When she returned with Eddie's grape, Mark raised his hand.

"Hey, servant," he said.

"Don't tell me," Kara snapped. "You want a grape, right?"

Mark shook his head. "Nope," he said. "I just remembered something. When I walked Chester after school, he pooped right in front of Mom's rosebushes, and I forgot to clean it up."

"Forgot? Yeah, right." Kara rolled her eyes. Mark and Todd were always getting in trouble for "forgetting" to clean up after the dog.

"Aha!" Eddie said. "That sounds like a job for our servant."

"Yeah," Todd said. "Servant Kara, go pick up that dog doo-doo."

"No way," Kara said. "It was Mark's

turn to walk him. It's his job to clean up after him."

Chip waggled one finger at her. "Are you going back on our deal?"

Kara's shoulders slumped. "No," she mumbled. "I'll go pick it up."

By the time she got back inside after cleaning up after the dog, the boys had disappeared from the kitchen. For a second Kara was relieved.

*Maybe they got bored and wandered off,* she thought. *After all, Mom's always talking about their short attention spans.*

But a second later the four boys rushed back into the kitchen.

"Oh, there you are, servant," Chip said. "It's about time you got back. We were waiting for you to clean up the table and then serve us our next course."

"Yeah," Mark said. "Goldfish crackers!"

"One at a time," Todd added.

Eddie grinned. "And when you're finished with that, I need you to wash my lucky gym socks. By hand, of course."

Kara sighed loudly. "Stupid dummies," she muttered.

"What was that?" Chip asked. "I thought I heard someone trying to back out of our deal."

"You should get your hearing checked," Kara snapped.

She could tell it was going to be a long three and a half days. *Oh well,* she thought as she started cleaning up the kitchen table. *At least I can spend my spare time thinking up ways to get my revenge once the sleepover is finished. . . .*

# ✳ 3 ✳

## Twin Trouble

The next day at school Kara was so tired she could hardly keep her eyes open. Her brothers had kept her up very late. They never seemed to run out of ideas for things they could order her to do. First she had to wash all their stinky gym socks by hand. Then they made her clean out under their beds and organize their closets. Her parents gave her a suspicious look when they caught her vacuuming Chip and Eddie's room. But they didn't ask too many questions.

When nine o'clock came, Kara thought she was finally safe. That was her weekday bedtime.

But Chip and Eddie sneaked in at eleven o'clock, after their parents were asleep, and woke Kara up again. They made her fix them a snack, then clean the mud off the bottoms of all their sneakers with an old toothbrush. She wasn't allowed to go back to bed until she'd cleaned out Eddie's pet lizards' cage. He hadn't cleaned it in more than a week, so it took a long time.

When her father came in to wake her for breakfast, Kara felt as if she'd been in bed for only five minutes. She almost fell asleep in her cereal two or three times, and her feet dragged during the whole walk to school.

All morning she did her best to keep her eyes open in class. It was a relief when recess came. She was pretty sure she wouldn't get in trouble for falling asleep during recess.

Kara followed her friends out to the playground. It was another beautiful autumn day. The sun was shining, and the air was crisp. It had rained the night before, and sunlight sparkled off the puddles on the blacktop. All over the playground, kids were running and playing and laughing.

But all Kara wanted to do was curl up in a ball and go to sleep.

"Want to play hopscotch?" Jo asked the others.

Kara yawned. "Maybe later," she mumbled. "Let's go on the swings first."

Sitting on a swing sounded a lot less tiring than playing hopscotch. Kara was trying not to let her friends see that anything was wrong. She didn't want them to know about her deal with her brothers. If they thought the boys might ruin the sleepover, they might not want to come.

Besides, it was kind of embarrassing. Why did she have to be the only one stuck with obnoxious brothers?

Taylor made a face. "We went on the swings yesterday," she said. "Let's do something more exciting."

"We could play jump rope," Emily said. "Does that sound okay, Kara?"

"Whatever," Kara snapped. "If you guys want to play jump rope, let's play jump rope."

She stomped off toward the equipment bins at the edge of the playground. That was where the jump ropes, balls, and other equipment was kept. She was so upset that she stomped right through a puddle and got her sneakers all wet.

Jo caught up to her a second later. "Hey," she said. "Are you okay? You've been acting weird all day."

Kara bit her lip. She should have known

Jo would notice that something was wrong. Jo noticed everything.

"It's nothing," Kara said. "Forget about it. Come on, we'd better go grab a jump rope before they're all taken."

She hurried off again. When she looked over her shoulder, she saw all three of her best friends trading a worried glance.

This time Taylor was the first one to catch up. "Yo, K," she said. "What's your deal today? No offense, but you're acting awfully cranky."

"Yeah," Emily added softly. "That's not like you, Kara. Is something wrong?"

"If there's something wrong, we should talk about it," Jo said. "Or are you not feeling well? Maybe you should go see the school nurse."

Taylor's eyes widened. "Ooh, I didn't even think of that," she said. "When I'm getting sick, I'm always totally cranky."

"Would you guys quit bugging me?"

Kara cried. "I'm not getting sick, okay? And there's nothing I want to talk about either. Isn't anyone allowed to just be tired around here?"

Her friends looked surprised at her outburst. Emily's blue eyes welled up with tears. She was sensitive that way.

Kara felt bad. She hated when Emily got upset.

"Excuse me," Kara mumbled. "I have to go to the bathroom."

She ran off before her friends could say anything. The playground monitor gave her a hall pass, and Kara went back inside.

The school hallway was quiet and echoey. All the students were either outside or sitting in class. Kara walked as slowly as she could toward the bathroom. Her damp sneakers made squeaking sounds against the tile floor.

She didn't really have to use the bathroom. So she just washed her hands instead, then dried them carefully. After that she took off her sneakers and held them under the hand dryer for a while.

Then she put her sneakers back on and just stood there staring at herself in the mirror. Her hazel eyes looked droopy and tired. Her skin looked pale, which made her freckles stand out more than normal. Even her red hair looked less springy than usual.

If she was this tired now, how was she going to survive two and a half more days of being her brothers' servant? Maybe it wasn't worth it.

Then she started imagining some of the things the boys could do to ruin her fun on Saturday. She shuddered. Being their servant was *definitely* worth it. She had to save the sleepover.

She stayed in the bathroom as long as she could. Finally, a fourth grader came in, and Kara decided it was time to leave.

She went back out to the playground. Her friends were watching some other girls play hopscotch.

"What took you so long?" Taylor asked. "We thought you fell in."

Emily peered at her, looking worried. "Are you sure you're not sick?"

Before Kara could answer, she heard shrieks and squeals from nearby. The first graders were pouring out onto the playground. Their recess started a few minutes before the second and third graders went back in.

"Kara! Kara!"

Kara winced. The twins were running toward her, shouting her name. Usually they pretended they didn't even know her. Kara liked it that way.

"Hi there, Carrottop Twins," Taylor greeted the boys. That was her favorite nickname for Mark and Todd. "What's up?"

"We want to go on the seesaw," Todd announced. "But first we want Kara to go clean off the seats with her shirt, in case they're dirty."

Taylor laughed. "Fat chance, Freckle Face," she said.

But Kara was already walking toward

the seesaw. "I'll wipe it off," she grumbled. "But I'm using my pant leg. This is a brand-new shirt."

"Whatever," Mark said. "Just hurry up."

Kara scowled at him. She wasn't happy that the twins were ordering her around in front of her friends. But if she didn't do as they said, they would tell Chip and Eddie. And then she could forget about having a fun sleepover.

Only one seesaw was free. Kara kneeled on one seat, rubbing it with the knees of her jeans. Then she did the other seat. She tried not to look at her friends. They were standing nearby, watching her.

The twins were watching too. "Okay, that's clean enough," Todd said. "But don't go anywhere. We might need you for something else."

"Yeah." Mark sat down on the low end of the seesaw. Then he looked down at his sneaker. "Hey, my shoe is untied. Come over here and tie it."

Kara clenched her fists. She wanted to rip Mark's shoe off and bonk him over the head with it. Instead, she forced herself to smile.

"Okay," she said. "Hold still. . . ."

She bent down and tied her brother's sneaker. Out of the corner of her eye, she could see her friends. They all looked astonished.

Just then the bell rang. That meant it was time for the older kids to go back inside.

"Oops," Kara said. "I have to go."

She hurried away before the boys could say anything. Her friends caught up with her halfway to the school door.

"Okay, what was that all about?" Taylor demanded.

Kara felt her face turn red. "Nothing," she mumbled.

But she knew it was no use playing dumb. Her friends weren't stupid. They could see that something strange was going on.

"Kara . . . ," Emily began softly.

Kara didn't even wait for her to finish. "Okay, okay!" she cried, throwing her hands into the air. "I might as well tell you. But you're not going to like it."

She quickly told them the whole story. By the time she'd finished, all three of her friends looked horrified and outraged.

"I can't believe they're doing this!" Emily exclaimed.

"Yeah." Jo shook her head. "That's pretty obnoxious, even for your brothers, Kara."

"You can't let them get away with this, K," Taylor declared.

Kara shrugged. "What else can I do?" she said. "If I don't go along with their stupid deal, they'll play practical jokes on us and be total jerks during our sleepover."

Taylor smiled. "So what?" she said. "How bad can it be? If they want to play that game, tell them to bring it on!"

# ✳ 4 ✳

## Enough Is Enough!

By the time school ended, Kara still wasn't sure what to think. Part of her agreed with Taylor. Maybe the best thing to do was plan their own prank to get back at the boys. That might teach them a lesson.

But another part of her was nervous. Taylor and the others didn't know just how obnoxious Kara's brothers could be.

"You guys don't understand," she told them when they were all walking out of the school building. "None of you knows what it's like to have brothers."

"I do," Jo said.

Kara had almost forgotten about Jo's brother, Alfonso. He was so much older that he seemed more like an uncle or cousin than a brother. Besides, he wasn't even around that much anymore. He and Jo's sister, Lydia, were both in college. That meant they lived in a different state for most of the year.

"Al doesn't count," Kara said. "He's not an immature dodo-head like my brothers." She took a deep breath. "Anyway, it doesn't matter. I can go along with their stupid deal for a few more days if it means saving the sleepover."

"Are you sure?" Emily looked doubtful.

Kara *wasn't* sure. She wasn't very good at going along with things she didn't like. And she definitely didn't like being her brothers' servant.

But she nodded. "I can do it," she said. "I *have* to. Besides, maybe my parents will catch them bossing me around. If they figure out what's going on, they might send all four of them to reform school before this weekend."

Her friends laughed. "That would be nice," Jo said. "But don't worry, Kara. Things will be okay either way."

"That's right," Taylor agreed. "If you have to break the deal and the boys go ahead with their threats, we're up for the challenge."

Emily nodded. "How bad could it be?"

"Bad." Kara shuddered. "Don't you remember the time they locked me in the basement and told the babysitter I ran away? Or the time they tricked me into eating a worm sandwich?"

Taylor waved one hand in the air. "Those pranks were totally lame," she said. "I'm sure we could come up with something much more creative."

"But only if we have to," Emily put in. She sounded kind of worried.

"Only if we have to," Jo agreed.

Taylor shrugged. "Sure," she said. "But if we have to, we have to. And those boys will be sorry they messed with us."

She didn't sound very worried at all. That made Kara feel a little bit better.

They were outside the school by now. Emily looked over at the curb where parents could pull up in their cars.

"There's my dad," she said. Emily's father was a teacher at the high school. He picked her up from school every day after he finished grading papers.

"I'd better go get on my bus," Jo said. "Good luck, Kara."

"Thanks. I'll need it." Kara waved as Emily and Jo hurried off in opposite directions.

"Ready to go?" Taylor asked.

Taylor and Kara both walked home from

school. Kara's house was just five blocks away, and Taylor's was a few blocks farther.

They joined a bunch of kids waiting on the curb. When the crossing guard waved them on, they all crossed the street.

"So what are we going to do at our sleepover?" Taylor asked. "Do you have lots of ideas?"

"Well, not *lots*," Kara said. She jumped over a puddle on the sidewalk. "I've been so busy doing everything my brothers say that I've barely had time to think about it. But Mom and Dad said they would rent us some movies, and—"

"Kara! Kara!"

It was the twins. They walked home from school too. Just like on the playground, they usually ignored her and walked with their own friends. But not today.

"What do you want?" Kara asked.

Mark and Todd grinned. "We want that big yellow leaf over there in the gutter,"

Mark said. "Go get it for us, servant Kara."

"You guys are really obnoxious, did you know that?" Kara grumbled. "I can't believe I'm related to you. Mom and Dad won't admit it, but I bet I'm adopted."

Taylor laughed. "I don't think so."

Kara knew she was right. All the Wyatt kids looked alike. They all had wavy red hair and lots of freckles.

Kara went over and picked up the yellow leaf. She held it out to the boys.

"Put it in your hair," Mark ordered.

"What?" Kara said.

Mark pointed to her head. "Put it in your hair. You know—like a decoration."

Kara looked around. All the other kids were at least half a block ahead of them. Nobody was looking at her except Taylor and the twins.

*I have to save the sleepover,* she thought.

Reaching up, she stuck the yellow leaf

into her thick red hair. Mark pointed and laughed.

"Kara's a tree!" he cried.

Meanwhile Todd pulled a granola bar out of his pocket. He held it out to Kara.

"Hey, servant Kara, open this for me," he said.

Kara grabbed the granola bar. "Do you want me to eat it for you too, you little twerp?"

"It's okay," Taylor whispered. "If you can't take it anymore, just quit. We can handle it."

"No." Hearing Taylor say that made Kara feel stronger. "It's okay." She unwrapped the granola bar and handed it back to Todd. "Here you go. Be careful not to choke on it."

For the next couple of blocks the twins continued to order Kara around. Taylor tried to help with some of the ridiculous tasks, but the boys wouldn't let her. They wanted Kara to do everything herself.

Another crossing guard waved them across Dogwood Street. "Only two blocks and you'll be home," Taylor whispered to Kara as they hurried across.

Kara shrugged. "Big deal," she said. "Chip and Eddie are there already, remember? That means twice as many jerky brothers to boss me around."

Todd hopped up onto the curb on the other side of the street. There was a big mud puddle at the edge of the sidewalk. Todd reached into his backpack and took out a baseball. He leaned over and dropped it into the puddle. It landed with a splash, sending mud flying everywhere.

"Servant Kara!" he cried. "My baseball fell. Pick it up for me."

Kara leaned over to pick up the wet, muddy baseball. She tried to use only her fingertips. She hated getting dirty. But she wasn't going to let the boys see that it bothered her.

"Here you go," she said, holding out the ball.

Todd wrinkled his nose. "Ew, it's all dirty," he said. "Servant Kara, wipe it off on your shirt."

"No way," Kara said. "I'll wipe it on my

jeans if you want. But I'm not using my new shirt to clean your stupid baseball."

Mark crossed his arms. "Didn't you hear him, servant Kara? He said to use your *shirt*."

"Use your shirt! Use your shirt!" Todd chanted.

Kara looked down at her new shirt. She could feel her face going red. Both boys were chanting now. They were so loud that some of the other kids were looking back at them curiously. Taylor was biting her lip, looking worried.

"Hurry up, servant!" Mark told Kara. "Otherwise we'll have to tell Chip you went back on our deal."

Enough was enough.

"Go ahead and tell him!" Kara yelled. She threw the ball at the boys. "The deal is off!"

# ✳ 5 ✳

## Breaking the Deal

Kara stomped off toward home. She didn't even stop when Taylor called her name. She was too furious to talk.

But Taylor caught up and grabbed her arm. "Hey, K," Taylor said. "Don't be upset. It'll be okay."

Kara glared at her. "That's easy for you to say," she cried. "You don't have to live with them!"

Just then the twins came running toward them. Kara clenched her fists. If they ordered her to do one more thing, she was going to push *them* into a mud puddle!

But the boys ran right past her. They made a beeline for their house, which was just a block away now.

"See?" Taylor said. "Looks like you scared them. Maybe they'll leave you alone now."

"Yeah, I wish," Kara muttered. "That would only happen in opposite land."

The two girls started walking again. "Look on the bright side," Taylor said. "At least now you don't have to do what they say anymore. You're free!"

"Look on the bright side?" In spite of her bad mood Kara smiled a little. "You sound like Emily."

Taylor laughed. "She must be rubbing off on me."

"Me too," Kara said. "Trying to go along with the boys' stupid deal sounds like something she would do. She always does her best to get along with people." She sighed. "But I should know better. Getting along with my brothers is hopeless."

They were almost to her house by now. Kara stopped on the sidewalk and looked up. Usually she loved coming home. Her house was built of brick, just like most of the others on the block. It wasn't as old as Emily's family's farmhouse, but it was a lot older than the homes in Jo's development. The paint on the shutters was starting to peel, and there were weeds in the flower beds, but the whole place looked happy and lived-in.

The inside was just as well-worn and well-loved as the outside. The rooms weren't as big as the ones in Taylor's house, but the ceilings were high and the windows let in lots of light. Kara's favorite part of the house was her cozy bedroom at the top of the attic stairs. She was the only one in the family who had her own room, since she was the only girl.

But today she dreaded going inside. What would be waiting for her in there?

Taylor smiled at her. "Hang in there," she said. "You only have to put up with them until Saturday. Then they won't have the slumber party to hold over your head anymore."

Kara said good-bye to Taylor and headed for the door. Inside she found all four of her brothers waiting for her in the front room.

"The twins told us what happened." Chip had his arms crossed over his chest. "Would you like to explain yourself, servant?"

"Don't call me that anymore," Kara shot back. "And I don't have to explain anything to you."

Eddie raised his eyebrows. "Did you hear that, Chip?" he said. "Our servant is talking back."

Chip shook his head. "Tsk, tsk," he said. "Now, Kara, I'm going to give you one last chance to apologize for this shocking behavior. Then we can get back to our deal."

Kara scowled. "I'm tired of bringing you snacks and washing your stinky socks. You can do it yourselves from now on."

"Oh yeah?" Mark cried. "You'd better do what we say, or else!"

"Forget it." Kara put her hands on her hips. "The deal is off."

Chip and Eddie traded a glance. "Okay, if that's how you feel about it," Chip said.

Eddie shrugged. "You'll be sorry."

"I'm already sorry," Kara snapped. "Sorry I have brothers!"

For the rest of the afternoon the boys did their best to drive Kara crazy. They whispered to one another whenever she walked by, and made funny faces every time she looked at them.

But that wasn't all. Kara was watching TV in her parents' room when she heard footsteps up on the third floor. She jumped up and ran upstairs.

"Hey, are you guys in my room?" she yelled. "You'd better not be in there!"

But the boys weren't in her room. They were in the other half of the attic. Eddie was carrying a big cardboard box.

"What are you doing?" Kara asked.

"Halloween is coming," Chip said. "So we decided to get out all our old monster masks."

"Halloween is weeks away," Kara said. "Why did you get them out now?"

Eddie set the box down at the top of the steps. "We just want to be prepared."

"Yeah," Mark said with a giggle.

"Prepared for anything," Todd added.

Kara stared at Mark's werewolf mask

lying near the top of the box. Emily was terrified of big, mean dogs. . . .

Later, Kara was coming in from walking Chester when she saw something scuttle under the coffee table in the front room. "Aaaah!" she screamed.

Eddie strolled into the room. "What's wrong?"

"I saw something crawl under there," Kara said. "It looked like . . . Wait a minute."

She bent down and peered under the table. Looking back at her was one of Eddie's pet lizards. When she turned around, she saw Chester sniffing at the second lizard. It was perched on the back of the sofa.

Eddie grinned. "Oh, did Bubba and Clyde startle you?" he said. "Sorry about that. I'm just letting them get some exercise."

Kara glared at him. She was used to the lizards by now. But when Eddie first got them, she had thought they were ugly and kind of scary. How would her friends feel if they saw the lizards walking around the house while they were there?

"I hope you're not planning on exercising them a lot in the next few days," she said. "Like this Saturday, for instance?"

"I don't know what you're talking about," Eddie said with a smirk.

By the time her parents got home, Kara was feeling jumpy and suspicious. Her head was spinning with all the possible pranks her brothers might pull at her sleepover. What if her friends never wanted to sleep over at her house again? What if they decided they didn't even want her in the Sleepover Squad anymore?

*I wish I could have kept up that stupid deal,* she thought. *I wish I wasn't so worried about what might happen on Saturday night.*

*But most of all, I wish I didn't have any brothers!*

# 6

## Waiting and Wondering

"You were totally right, Emmers," Taylor said happily. "Fall is great!"

She took a big bite of the doughnut she was holding. Powdered sugar poofed out from the doughnut and onto Taylor's chin.

Kara laughed. "Hey, Taylor, you look like you have a white beard."

It was Saturday, and the four members of the Sleepover Squad were at Thompson Orchards. That was an orchard a few miles from Emily's house. Every autumn it was open to the public for apple picking, hayrides, and other fun fall activities. Emily's father had picked all the girls up and driven them there. In a little while he would drop them off at Kara's house for the sleepover.

"Can we go on the pony rides again?" Emily asked.

"Sure," Taylor said. "I want to ride the spotted one this time."

"A spotted pony is called a pinto," Emily said.

Emily knew a lot about horses. Her bedroom was filled with toy horses and horse books. Kara knew that Emily wanted to take riding lessons more than anything else in the world. But her parents still thought she was too young.

"We still have to try the corn maze, too," Jo said. "It looks like fun."

Emily nodded. "I almost forgot about that," she said. "Should we do that next?"

"Let's finish our doughnuts first, then do the pony rides," Jo said. "We should still have plenty of time for the maze."

Kara nodded along with the others. She was having fun at the orchard. But at the same time, everything they did reminded her of what might be waiting for them when they got back to her house. While they were picking apples, she wondered if the boys were at home hiding rotten bananas in her sleeping bag. When she felt the stiff hay poking her in the legs during the hayride, it reminded her of a lizard's claws walking on her in her sleep. As she took a sip of apple cider, she imagined her brothers pouring salt water or liquid soap into the orange juice carton.

Her friends finished eating. Kara popped the last bite of doughnut into her mouth and wiped the sugar off her fingers. Then she zipped up her jacket a little tighter. It was sunny, but chilly. She jammed her hands into her pockets and followed her friends toward the pony rides.

*The sleepover hasn't even started yet, and my brothers are already ruining my fun!* she thought, feeling a little grumpy.

When the girls finished their pony rides, Emily's father was waiting for them. "Almost ready to go?" he asked. "I told Kara's parents I'd have you there by three."

"Not yet, Daddy," Emily said. "We didn't go in the corn maze yet."

"Okay." Mr. McDougal smiled. "Go on and do the maze—as long as Kara doesn't mind putting off the start of her sleepover a few more minutes."

"No way," Kara said. "I don't mind at all."

The girls ran over to the corn maze. It was built out of tall cornstalks and straw bales. There was an entrance at one end, and an exit at the other end, with lots of twists and turns and dead ends in between.

Anyone who made it through without help got a free apple.

There were a few other kids in the maze when the girls entered. The girls could hear them laughing and yelling, but they couldn't see them. A few feet from the entrance the path split in two.

"This way," Jo said. She pointed down the right-hand path. "I bet this is the way."

"Only one way to find out!" Taylor grinned and charged down the path. Jo and Emily were right behind her.

Kara trailed behind the others. She was still thinking about her brothers. What were they doing right now?

"Dead end!" Taylor yelled. The girls had just turned a corner and found a wall of straw bales in front of them.

"Oops," Jo said. "Guess my bet was wrong."

"That's okay." Emily smiled and shrugged. "I was going to guess this way too."

Just then Jo looked at Kara. "Hey," she said. "Are you okay? You're being kind of quiet."

Kara didn't want to make her friends nervous about the sleepover. But she couldn't keep her worries to herself for another second.

"It's my stupid brothers," she blurted out.

"I'm sure they're at home right now setting up all kinds of crazy practical jokes!"

Taylor reached out and put an arm around her. "Don't worry," she said. "We'll deal with them later."

"Yeah," Jo added. "Don't let them ruin your fun now."

Kara sighed loudly. "But I can't help it! They could be doing anything."

"So what?" Taylor said. "No matter what lame stuff they do to us, we'll come up with something ten times better to get back at them."

"I guess you're right." Kara forced herself to smile.

But inside she wasn't so sure. What could her nice friends do against the most obnoxious boys in the world?

Half an hour later Mr. McDougal dropped the girls off at the curb in front of Kara's house. "Have fun, kids," he said.

Emily, Taylor, and Jo said good-bye and thanked him for the ride. But Kara was distracted. She'd just spotted her brothers. They were raking leaves in the front yard.

"Just ignore them," Kara whispered to her friends as they started toward the house. "Don't even look at them."

"Hi there, girls!" Chip called loudly as they walked past.

"Hi," Emily called back. Then she smiled sheepishly at Kara. "Sorry," she said. "I was just being polite."

Soon the girls were inside. "Should we watch a movie?" Kara asked. "Mom and Dad rented a bunch for us. We could make microwave popcorn — Mom got the movie-theater-butter kind."

"We can do that when it gets dark," Taylor said. "Maybe we should go outside for a while first." Taylor loved being outside. She got restless if she had to stay inside for too long.

Kara bit her lip. "Outside?" she said. "But my brothers are out there."

Taylor frowned. "Are you going to let those boys stop us from doing what we want?"

"We could do both." Emily held up one of the DVDs. "This one's only half an hour long. We could watch it and still have lots of time to play outside before dinnertime."

"That's a great idea," Jo agreed.

Kara nodded. Maybe by the time the video finished, the boys would have wandered off somewhere.

But the DVD was only half over when she heard the front door bang open. She looked up and saw all four of her brothers walking in. They all paused by the door just long enough to shrug off their jackets and hang them up on the coatrack.

She clutched her popcorn bowl closer. What would they do now? Were they planning to throw leaves in the girls' hair? Or were their pockets full of spiders? Or did they have something even more horrible in mind?

# ✳ 7 ✳

## Gotcha!

Chip took a step closer. Kara held her breath.

"Excuse me," Chip said. "Can I have a handful of popcorn? Raking is hungry work."

"Sure." Taylor held out the bowl she was sharing with Emily. "Have some of ours."

"Thanks." Chip scooped up some popcorn. Then he glanced around at his brothers. "Come on, guys. Let's go down in the rec room and leave them alone."

"Okay," Eddie said. "I call first turn on the pinball machine."

"No way!" Todd cried. He and Mark raced ahead toward the basement door. A moment later all the boys had disappeared down the stairs.

Kara was so surprised she could hardly talk for a second. "What's going on?" she exclaimed. "Why didn't they do anything obnoxious?"

Jo reached for some popcorn. "Maybe they're afraid they'll get in trouble."

"No way," Kara said. "Mom and Dad are way out in the back watering the garden. This was their perfect chance to get us."

"I know!" Emily's face lit up. "Maybe this *is* their big prank! Maybe their plan is to drive you crazy and make you worry all night while they do nothing."

Kara shrugged. "Maybe," she said. "But I doubt it. My brothers aren't that clever."

The others returned their attention

to the video. But Kara kept staring at the basement door. What were the boys really plotting down there?

"That was great!" Taylor said when the video ended a few minutes later. "Ready to go outside now?"

"Okay," Kara said. "But first maybe we should set up our sleeping area for later."

Even Taylor agreed with that. It was always fun to lay out their sleeping bags and pillows.

Kara led the way up to the second floor, then down the hall toward the attic steps.

Chip and Eddie's bedroom door was closed. But Emily peeked into the twins' room as she passed. "I think you were too worried about your brothers, Kara," she said. "They probably won't do anything that bad tonight."

"Yeah," Taylor said. "They probably realized they shouldn't mess with the

Sleepover Squad, or they'd be sorry."

Kara smiled weakly. She hoped her friends were right. But she still wasn't so sure.

"I hope there's room for all of us on your floor, Kara," Jo said as they started up the narrow steps.

"There is," Kara said. "Mom helped me clean up yesterday. We put some of my projects away for now."

Kara liked to create dioramas, sculpt things out of clay, build model planes and houses, and do all sorts of other art projects. Usually there were at least two or three of her projects spread out on her desk and floor at a time. Since her room wasn't very big, the projects didn't leave much space for anything else.

At the top of the stairs was a tiny landing. Two doors opened off it. One led to the storage part of the attic. The other one opened into Kara's room.

Kara reached for the knob. "Welcome to my . . . ," she began. Then she frowned.

"What's wrong?" Jo asked.

"The doorknob's all slippery." Kara lifted her hand to her nose and sniffed. "Butter!"

She grabbed the knob tighter and opened the door. "Wait!" Taylor yelled from right behind her. "Don't step forward!"

Kara looked down. There were at least a dozen eggs lined up just inside the doorway. If Taylor hadn't stopped her, Kara would have stepped right on one.

She clenched her fists. "I told you guys my brothers were up to no good!" she cried. "Look at poor Chester!"

The dog was sitting in the middle of Kara's bed. The only way to recognize him was by his wagging tail. He was wearing a hideous green and black monster mask that made him look like a creature from another planet.

Emily giggled as she stepped carefully over the eggs. "Um, interesting posters, Kara," she said. "Did you redecorate just for us?"

As Kara looked around, her heart sank. Her cozy little room looked like a different place. The boys had replaced the nice pictures on her walls with their own ugly wrestling posters and photos cut out of magazines—photos of toilets, bugs, and snakes.

"Do you think they messed with our stuff?" Taylor asked, leaping forward toward the pile of suitcases and sleeping bags at the foot of Kara's bed. Mr. McDougal had dropped off their things on the way to the orchard.

"I don't know," Kara said grimly. "But be careful."

Jo zipped open her suitcase and made a face. "Ugh," she said. "There are worms in my bag!"

"Ew!" Taylor cried, leaning over to look.

"Don't squish them," Emily said. "Worms are good. I'll help you get them out in a second. Then we can put them in the flower beds outside."

She and Taylor each unzipped their bags.

"No way!" Taylor shrieked. "Those dorks put a bunch of stinky socks in here. All my stuff is going to smell!"

"They took everything out of mine and filled it with rocks," Emily said. "Where are my pajamas?"

Kara sat down on the edge of her bed. She put her head in her hands. This was even worse than she'd feared.

Just then she heard a giggle from the doorway. She looked up and saw Mark's face peeking in. A second later Eddie appeared behind him. He was grinning.

"You jerks!" Kara screamed. "I'll get you for this!"

She leaped up and raced for the door.

Her heart was pounding, and her head was throbbing with rage. She was ready to strangle all four boys with her bare hands.

Taylor caught her by the arm. "Wait!" she said. "Kara, calm down a second."

"How can I calm down?" Kara was so furious that there were tears in her eyes. She waved a hand at the chaos around her. "Look at what they did!"

She wriggled to get away. But Taylor grabbed her by both shoulders. She was taller and stronger than Kara, so Kara had to stop.

"Hold on," Taylor said quietly. "Listen to me, Kara. There's a better way to get back at them. . . ."

## ✺ 8 ✺

### Get Mad or Get Even?

For a few minutes Kara didn't want to listen to Taylor. All she wanted was to pound her brothers. Or maybe just dunk their heads in the toilet until they begged for mercy.

"You guys better run!" she screamed when she heard them racing off down the steps. "You better run all the way to Timbuktu if you don't want me to kill you!"

She tried to break free of Taylor's grip. But Jo stepped forward to help Taylor.

"Settle down, Kara," Jo said. "Going loco won't fix anything. It's exactly what they want."

"Let me go," Kara cried. "If you don't want me to kill them, at least let me go get Mom and Dad. When they see this mess, *they'll* kill them!"

"You don't need to tattle," Taylor said. "That will only make things worse."

"What are you talking about?" Kara cried. "How could things get worse? They ruined our sleepover!"

Emily put a hand on her arm. "No, they didn't."

Kara blinked. Suddenly she realized something. Her friends didn't look nearly as upset as she was. If she didn't know better, she might even think they were having . . . fun. None of them were crying or calling their parents to pick them up.

"I don't get it," she said. "Aren't you guys mad about this?"

"Well, I'm not exactly thrilled about cleaning worms out of my underwear," Jo said with a laugh. "But we all figured your brothers would make trouble."

"Yeah," Emily said. "Sort of the way we figured the sun would set tonight and rise again in the morning."

Taylor and Jo giggled. "No," Taylor said. "We were *more* sure about her brothers than we were about the sun."

Kara stared at them. Then she looked around her room. She couldn't believe it. Her friends didn't even have obnoxious brothers. They weren't used to these sorts of pranks.

"So you aren't so upset that you never want to come over again?" she asked.

"Don't be silly," Jo said. "It's not that big a deal."

Emily nodded. "The only thing we're upset about is that *you're* so upset."

"Yeah." Taylor grinned. "And don't

worry, we're going to make them pay for that!"

"Do you want a tissue?" Emily asked Kara. "I have some in the outside pocket of my suitcase . . . or at least I did. There might be rocks in there now. But I can check."

"Thanks." Kara sniffled. She realized that tears had been streaming down her face while she screamed at her brothers.

Emily reached for her bag. There was a big pocket on the outside. When she unzipped the flap, something inside the pocket moved.

"Eep!" Emily squeaked, jumping back quickly.

A second later a small, scaly green head popped out and looked around. It was one of Eddie's lizards.

Kara sighed. "Sorry, Em."

Emily swallowed hard.

"It's—it's okay," she said. "Um, can one of you help me get it out of there, though?"

A little while later Kara raced down the basement steps. Her brothers were in the rec room. Chip and Eddie were playing air hockey. The twins were sprawled on the beat-up brown sofas reading comic books.

"Hey, look who's here," Eddie said when he spotted Kara. "How did you like our decorating job in your room?"

"Yeah, how many eggs did you step on, Kara?" Mark asked.

"Did you find the worms?" Todd added. "That was my idea."

"Never mind all that!" Kara cried, her eyes wide. She waved her hands to shut them up. "Listen, this is serious!"

"What?" Chip looked suspicious.

"It's Emily!" A few tears squeezed out of the corners of Kara's eyes. "When she found Bubba in her suitcase, she got really upset and ran outside crying."

"It was Clyde, not Bubba," Eddie corrected. "Bubba is in your sock drawer."

"She really ran out like that?" Chip looked sort of guilty, but then he shrugged. "Well, so what? We can't help it if your friend is a big wimp, just like you."

"No, no, that's not the problem," Kara cried. "When she ran out, she left the front door open behind her, and Chester got out and ran off down the street. Now he's missing!"

# ✳ 9 ✳

## The Last Laugh

"No way!" Chip sounded panicky. "Come on, guys. We've got to find Chester!"

They raced up the stairs. Kara hurried after them. She reached the front room just in time to see the boys grab their jackets from the coatrack by the door. They ran out without another word, slamming the door behind them.

Kara turned and walked around the couch. Her friends were kneeling behind it.

"You can come out now," Kara said. "They're gone."

"We heard." Taylor stood up and grinned. "We could hear you all the way in the basement too."

Emily nodded. "You're a great actress, Kara," she said. "If I didn't know better, I would have thought you were really upset."

Kara giggled. "Thanks. Where's Chester?"

"We shut him in your parents' room so he wouldn't bark when the boys ran out," Jo said. "I'll go let him out now."

"Yeah," Taylor said. "He won't want to miss what happens next!"

Soon Jo returned with Chester. Kara walked over and grabbed his leash from the coatrack.

"Let's go out on the porch and wait," she suggested. "Chester can sit with us."

"Good idea," Taylor said.

Soon the four girls were sitting on the front porch. Kara and Jo were on the swing. Emily was sitting on the floor scratching Chester's ears. Even though she was afraid of most big dogs, she liked Chester. He was too lazy and gentle to be scary.

Taylor was pacing back and forth at the top of the porch steps. "It sounds like a lot of kids are still outside playing," she said. "That's good."

Kara nodded. It was still a little before dinnertime. A lot of people in the neighborhood were outside enjoying the nice autumn afternoon. A group of teenagers was shooting baskets in the Farleys' driveway two doors down, and some younger kids were jumping in leaf piles in one of the yards across the street. The sounds of kids talking and playing came from every direction.

And soon, another sound came from

every direction. "Listen," Taylor said. "I think it's working."

There was a loud shriek of laughter from down the block. Then another, and another.

Soon, all that the girls could hear was laughing. A moment later Kara's parents appeared from around the corner of the house. Mrs. Wyatt was wearing gardening gloves, and Mr. Wyatt had the newspaper tucked under one arm.

"What's going on out there?" Mr. Wyatt asked the girls. "We were in the backyard, and we heard all the racket."

"I don't know, Dad," Kara said with a grin. "Sounds like something funny is happening out there."

Her friends all burst out laughing. Mr. and Mrs. Wyatt looked suspicious. They traded a curious glance.

Before they could ask any more questions, there was another shout of laughter.

This time it came from the basketball play-ers. A moment later Chip, Eddie, Mark, and Todd raced toward the porch.

"Hi, boys!" Taylor called loudly, waving to them. "Look, we found Chester."

Chester barked and wagged his tail.

Chip leaped up onto the porch and glared at the girls. He was red-faced and out of breath, just like the other boys. They were all carrying their jackets bundled up in their arms.

"You guys did this, didn't you?" Chip cried. "Stupid jerks!"

"Hold on there, champ," Mr. Wyatt said sternly. "Don't yell at your sister and her friends."

"But look what they did!" Eddie held up his jacket.

Kara put a hand over her mouth to hold back her giggles. A big sign was pinned to the back of Eddie's jacket with at least a dozen safety pins. It said I PICK MY NOSE.

Chip, Mark, and Todd held up their jackets too. All of them had similar signs. Chip's said I'M AFRAID OF GIRLS. Mark's said I HAVE COOTIES. Todd's said I EAT DOG POOP.

"Everyone in the neighborhood saw us walking around like this!" Eddie exclaimed. He sounded outraged.

"*They* did it!" Todd pointed to Kara and the other girls.

"Yeah," Chip said. "They knew we'd rush out so fast we wouldn't notice until it was too late."

Mark scowled and tried to rip his sign off his jacket. "You guys are in big trouble now," he said. "We caught you red-handed."

For a second Kara was worried. What if her parents took the boys' side?

"I see," her father said slowly. He glanced over at his wife. "And just why were you rushing out so fast, boys?"

"We thought Chester ran away," Todd said.

"And why would you think that?" Mrs. Wyatt asked. "He's sitting right here."

"Yeah, but Kara told us Emily let him out," Eddie said.

"That doesn't sound like something Emily would do," his father said. "She's a very careful and responsible girl."

Emily blushed. "Thank you, Mr. Wyatt."

"Ask them why they thought Em let him out," Kara said.

"Good question," Mr. Wyatt said. "Boys?"

Since Mr. and Mrs. Wyatt were both engineers, that meant they were very logical people. Jo was a logical person too. She was the one who had said Kara's parents would figure out what had really happened. And she was right. A few minutes later Kara's parents had the whole story.

"Okay, so maybe we played a few pranks," Eddie said with a frown. "But their prank was just mean!"

"Maybe a little." Mrs. Wyatt looked as if she were trying not to laugh. "But somehow I doubt they would have done it if you hadn't played all those jokes on them first."

"Yes," Mr. Wyatt added. "I think we can call this one a draw." He smiled. "Although, boys, you really ought to be ashamed of yourselves. The girls' prank was much more clever than yours."

"Thanks, Dad," Kara said.

"You're welcome." Her father winked at her. "But that doesn't mean I want to encourage this sort of thing in the future."

"Don't worry, Mr. W," Taylor said. "We won't be playing any more pranks. Unless absolutely necessary, that is." She turned and grinned at the boys.

They scowled back at her. "Whatever," Chip muttered. "Can we go inside now?"

Kara laughed as they slunk away. She was pretty sure the kids in the neighborhood would be talking about this prank for a long time. She was also pretty sure that she and her friends would be able to enjoy the rest of the sleepover without any further mischief from her brothers.

At least *this* time . . .

# Slumber Party Project:
# Joking Around

Some pranks are mean, but some can be fun. Try these tricks to liven up your next sleepover.

1. Icky Ice: Buy some fake bugs or other creepy crawlies at the toy store or dollar store. Get an adult to help you freeze them into ice cubes. Then serve them to your friends and wait for the screams!

2. Slippery Sink: Put petroleum jelly or butter on the handles of the bathroom sinks—right before it's time for your

friends to brush their teeth. Then stand back and laugh when they try to turn on the water!

3. Rainbow Milk: Ask your parents to buy milk in a cardboard carton (not a see-through jug). Put a few drops of food coloring in the milk (red, green, or blue work well). Then serve your friends cereal for breakfast, and watch their faces when they pour in the colorful milk!

# P. J. DENTON

# Sleepover Squad

## #4 Keeping Secrets

Illustrated by Julia Denos

# 1

## The Spring Spelling Bee

Jo Sanchez took a deep breath. Her palms felt damp and warm, so she wiped them on her pants. She wondered if the other kids on the stage of the Oak Tree Elementary School auditorium were getting nervous too.

"Min Choi, you're next," Ms. Paolini, the fifth-grade English teacher, called out.

Ms. Paolini was running the Spring Spelling Bee. She was standing at one end of the stage, reading out the words for the students to spell.

Jo watched fourth grader Min Choi step to the microphone. Ms. Paolini smiled at Min.

"Min, your word is 'satellite,'" the teacher said.

Min slowly spelled out the word. But Jo didn't pay attention. Instead, she peered down the row of chairs on either side of her. Most of them were empty now, though all of them had been full just a short while ago. She could hardly believe it—she was the last third grader left on stage! The second-to-last one, Tammy Tandrich, had been knocked out of the spelling bee in the last round. She'd misspelled the word "achieve." Now the only people left were Jo and seven other kids. All of the others were fourth or fifth graders.

Next Jo looked out into the audience. It was hard to see anything out there since the spotlights were shining straight at the stage. That left the rest of the auditorium in shadow. But Jo was pretty sure she could see her mother sitting a few rows back. She wished her father could be there too. But he was a doctor, and he couldn't leave his patients in the middle of the day.

Min finished spelling her word. "That's correct," Ms. Paolini told her. "Good job. Now it's Jo's turn again. Ms. Sanchez, please step forward."

Jo felt a funny, jumpy sensation in her stomach. Her friends were always teasing her because she never looked nervous, not even before a big test. She tried to tell them she still *felt* nervous sometimes. But she wasn't sure they believed her.

She brushed her shoulder-length dark hair out of her face and walked to the microphone. Then, looking over at Ms. Paolini, Jo waited for her next word.

"Whoooo! Go, Jo-Jo!" someone shouted from the audience.

The whole audience started laughing, and Jo smiled. She looked down and spotted her three best friends in the front row. All three of them had been in the spelling bee too. Each time someone got knocked out by spelling a word wrong, he or she went and sat down in the first section of the audience.

Taylor Kent was the one who'd yelled out. Taylor was very smart, but she was also very impatient. She'd sped through the spelling of the word "neighbor" without stopping to remember that it was supposed to have the letter *g* in it.

Beside Taylor, Kara Wyatt was laughing and waving to Jo. Kara wasn't a very good speller, so it was no surprise that she'd been knocked out early. She'd barely even *tried* to spell the word "geography" before giggling and giving up.

Emily McDougal was sitting on Kara's other side. Emily was looking over at Mr. Mackey, the music teacher, who was sitting at the end of their row. Emily hated causing a scene or getting in trouble, so she looked kind of nervous. A lot of things made Emily nervous. For one thing, she always got nervous when she had to stand up and talk in front of other people. Jo was pretty sure that was why Emily had messed up the word "exercise" a couple of rounds earlier. Normally, Emily was one of the best spellers in the third grade.

Mr. Mackey was laughing along with everyone else. "That's enough, Miss Kent," he called down the row.

Ms. Paolini smiled at Jo. "Now that your cheering section has settled down, let's continue," she said. "Since this is the Spring Spelling Bee, the next round will consist of words that have to do with spring. Your word is 'sprout.'"

Jo nodded and thought for a moment. She heard the word "sprout" all the time at Emily's house. Emily's mother ran an organic gardening business. This time of year, all the counters and tables at the McDougal house were filled with sprouting plants.

The trouble was, Jo wasn't sure how to

spell "sprout." It sounded like it might have a *w* in it. But that didn't seem quite right.

*It rhymes with "out,"* she thought. *So maybe it's spelled like that too.*

She took another few seconds to think about that. She didn't want to make a mistake by rushing.

"Sprout," she said at last. "S-P-R-O-U-T. Sprout?"

She held her breath, glancing over at Ms. Paolini. The teacher was smiling.

"Correct," she said. "Very good, Jo."

The audience clapped. Jo returned to the line of chairs at the back of the stage. She was relieved. That had been a hard word.

"Good job," Min whispered.

"Thanks," Jo whispered back.

It was Charles Phan's turn next. He jumped out of his chair so fast that he knocked it over. That was normal for Charles. He had a lot of energy.

"I'm ready," he yelled into the microphone. "Lay it on me, Ms. Paolini."

Everyone laughed, including Jo. Charles always made people laugh. He was one of the most hyper boys in the fourth grade. He was also one of the smartest.

Charles spelled his word, "daffodil," correctly. But the next two people got theirs wrong.

"Wow, this is a hard round," Min whispered to Jo, sounding nervous. "I hope my word is easy."

"Amy Robinson is next," Jo whispered back. "She's the smartest kid in the fifth grade. She'll probably get hers right."

Min nodded. "She won the last three spelling bees, remember?" she said. "The one in the fall this year, and both of the ones last year."

Jo's guess was correct. Amy got her word right. So did two other fifth graders, along with Min.

In the next round Jo got a word she knew—"guitar." She spelled it carefully and then sat down. Charles and Amy got their words right too. But Min and the two fifth graders got theirs wrong. That left only three people on stage—Charles, Amy, and Jo.

"It looks like we're down to our final three," Ms. Paolini said before starting the next round. "Congratulations, you three. And may the best speller win!"

Jo glanced over at the two older kids. She could hardly believe she was in the final three. Her friends might not think she ever got nervous, but she was definitely nervous now!

Amy was going first in this round. Jo watched the fifth grader walk to the microphone.

"Amy, your word is 'surgery,'" Ms. Paolini said.

Amy looked over at the teacher.

"Could you repeat that word, please?" she asked.

Even though Jo was sitting behind her, she could tell that Amy was nervous. She guessed that Amy wasn't sure how to spell her word.

Sure enough, Amy spelled it wrong. "I'm sorry, Amy," Ms. Paolini said. She spelled the word correctly, then asked Amy to come over and stand beside her.

Charles was next. He got his word wrong too.

"Your turn, Jo," Ms. Paolini said. "If you get this right, you win. If not, all three of you get to try again."

"But no pressure!" Charles called out with a laugh. He and Amy were both standing at the side of the stage near Ms. Paolini, waiting to see if Jo spelled her word correctly.

Jo stepped to the microphone. Her hands were shaking a little, and her head felt funny. What if she got her word wrong? She didn't want to look stupid.

"Ready?" Ms. Paolini asked. "Jo, your word is 'choir.'"

Jo smiled. Suddenly, she felt much less nervous. It was a pretty hard word to spell, but not for her. She was a member of her church choir—she definitely knew how to spell that word!

"Choir," she said confidently. "C-H-O-I-R."

She paused for a moment to think it over once more before making it official. She definitely didn't want to make a stupid mistake.

"Choir," she finished at last.

Ms. Paolini smiled. "Correct!" she said. "We have a winner!"

## * 2 *

## A Surprising Prize

"Way to go, Jo!" Kara cheered loudly as Jo stepped down from the stage. Kara even did a little jump and kick, just like the real cheerleaders at the high school football games. Her wavy red hair bounced around her face, falling over her eyes.

Emily and Taylor rushed forward to hug Jo. They both looked just as excited as Kara.

"That was so awesome!" Taylor exclaimed, her greenish gold eyes sparkling. "You

looked as cool as a cucumber up there. We should start calling you Super Jo!"

Emily giggled. "Super Jo, the super speller," she said.

"Thanks, guys." Jo could hardly believe she'd just won the Spring Spelling Bee. She'd beaten all those fourth and fifth graders—even Amy Robinson!

It made her feel good but also a little bashful. She was used to getting praise and attention from teachers because of her good grades. But this was different. It seemed as if the whole school was staring at her and cheering.

"Hey, Jo," someone called. "Congratulations."

Jo turned and saw that it was Amy Robinson. The older girl was smiling at her.

"Thanks." Jo felt more bashful than ever now. Fifth graders like Amy hardly ever talked to third graders. "You did really well too."

"Thanks. Well, I'd better go." Amy waved and hurried away toward her fifth-grade friends.

Kara watched her go. "Wow," she joked. "We'd better watch out. Now that Jo is friends with fifth graders, she probably won't want to hang out with us boring old third graders anymore."

"No way!" Jo said immediately. "I would never abandon the Sleepover Squad."

The Sleepover Squad was a club the four of them—Jo, Emily, Kara, and Taylor—had formed the previous spring. Whenever they could, they all got together and had sleepover parties at one of their houses.

Taylor clapped her hands. "That gives me a great idea," she said. "Why don't we have a sleepover to celebrate your big win? We haven't had one in a while."

Emily nodded. "I could ask my parents if we could do another campout in our tent."

Kara wrapped her freckled arms around herself and pretended to shiver. "A camp-out?" she said. "I know it's spring, but it's still way too cold out for camping. Maybe I can have it at my house instead. We can lock my brothers in the basement so they won't bug us."

Just then Jo's mother rushed over, smiling proudly. *"Buen hecho,* Jo!" she cried.

Her dark brown eyes, which looked just like Jo's, were dancing with excitement.

"Thanks, Mom," Jo said. She looked at her friends. "She just said 'well done.'" When her mother got excited, she sometimes forgot that not everyone could understand Spanish. Jo's whole family spoke both Spanish and English.

"*Gracias,*" Taylor said. She didn't really speak Spanish. But she'd learned how to say a few Spanish words, such as the one that meant "thank you," from her housekeeper.

Jo's mother squeezed Jo tightly. "Ready to head home?" she asked. "I can't wait to call your father and tell him about this."

The spelling bee had taken place during the last period of the day. Any parents who had come to watch could take their kids home now that it was over, even if the kids normally rode the school bus, like Jo.

"Sure, I guess." Jo wanted to stay with her friends and keep talking about their next sleepover. But she could tell her mother was eager to get home. Party planning would just have to wait.

Jo's father wasn't home when they got there, but he walked in an hour and a half later while Jo was setting the table for dinner.

"I made it!" he called out, walking across the dining room and into the kitchen. He hung up his jacket on the hook near the back door, then hurried back into the dining room. "So tell me, Jo—what was your winning word?"

He already knew Jo had won the spelling bee. Mrs. Sanchez had called him at the office to tell him that, and to find out what time he'd be home for dinner.

Jo carefully set down the stack of three white china plates she was holding. "It was 'choir,'" she told her father. "I bet they didn't know that would be such an easy word for me."

"It's not an easy word," he said, reaching over to give her a hug. "You're just a very smart girl. Exactly like your old papa."

"Thanks, Daddy." Jo giggled and hugged him back. As usual he smelled like a combination of lime aftershave, soap, and rubbing alcohol. His bristly chin tickled her forehead a little. "But Mom said I got my brain from her side of the family."

"She did, did she?" Dr. Sanchez straightened up and glanced at his wife. Mrs. Sanchez was standing in the doorway polishing a handful of silverware with a rag. "Interesting, very interesting."

Mrs. Sanchez ignored his comment. "Get those shoes off, Hector," she said. "You're tracking dirt all over my clean floors. Dinner's almost ready—we're having all of Jo's favorite foods to celebrate."

"Hamburgers and baked squash, eh?" Dr. Sanchez said.

Jo shrugged. "I wanted crab cakes, too,"

she said. "But Mom didn't have time to go over to the seafood shop this afternoon."

Her father chuckled. "Sounds like a delicious meal even without the crab cakes. But I'll have to eat fast," he said. "I need to go back to the office for a little while after dinner and take care of some paperwork."

Dr. Sanchez was a partner in a busy ear, nose, and throat medical practice. He often had to work on evenings and weekends as well as during the day. Sometimes he didn't even make it home for dinner. Jo was glad he could eat dinner with them tonight.

"Everything is just about ready," Mrs. Sanchez said. "Let's eat!"

Half an hour later, Jo had just finished her last few bites of squash when the phone rang. Her mother answered in English, then immediately switched to Spanish. A moment later she handed the phone to Jo.

"It's Grandpapa Sanchez," she said. "He wants to congratulate you."

Jo smiled and took the phone. Her grandfather lived in a town about ten miles away. Jo and her parents went to visit him at least a couple of times a month. Jo's aunt and uncle lived there too, so each visit was like a family reunion.

"*Hola,*" Jo said into the phone. Grandpapa Sanchez had been born in Mexico. He spoke English pretty well, but he still spoke Spanish better.

Jo talked to her grandfather for a few minutes while her parents cleared the table. Grandpapa Sanchez wanted to hear all about the spelling bee. He asked her to tell him every word she had to spell. Luckily, Jo remembered them all. She had a very good memory.

She hung up a few minutes later. When she turned around, she saw her parents sitting at the table watching her.

"Your mother and I have been talking, *mi cara,*" Dr. Sanchez said. "We have a great idea."

"What is it?" Jo wandered over and sat down. She wondered if her parents were going to tell her they were planning to fix crab cakes for dinner that weekend. Her mother liked crab cakes almost as much as Jo did.

But what her mother said next had nothing to do with crab cakes.

"We know you've been wanting to host

one of your sleepovers with your friends," Mrs. Sanchez said.

Jo nodded. She was the only one in the Sleepover Squad who hadn't had a party at her house yet. She had asked her parents about it several times. They had never exactly said no. But they had never exactly said yes, either. Jo knew they weren't very excited about the idea of having a sleepover at their house. They were a little older than her friends' parents, and they liked their house to be clean, neat, and quiet. At least that was what they always said when Jo asked if they could get a dog.

"Well," her father went on, "in honor of your big win today, we decided you can have a slumber party here this weekend if you want to."

Jo gasped. "I definitely want to!" she cried. "Thanks, you guys!"

She was so thrilled that she felt like

doing cartwheels, like Taylor probably would, or jumping up and down and giggling, like Kara. Instead, she just gave both of her parents big hugs.

"May I be excused?" she asked. "I want to go call my friends and tell them right now."

Taylor, Kara, and Emily were just as excited as Jo was. "This is perfect!" Emily exclaimed when she heard the news. "We were just trying to figure out where to have our next party, remember? Your parents must have read our minds!"

Jo laughed. She didn't believe in mind reading. But she knew Emily liked learning about strange things like that in some of the books she was always reading for fun.

"I'd better get off the phone," she told Emily. "I want to start making a list of stuff to do. Saturday is only four days away, and there's a lot of planning to do before then!"

# ✳ 3 ✳

## Making Plans

When Jo's bus got to school the next day, she was one of the first ones off. She couldn't wait to talk to her friends about all the plans she'd made.

Taylor and Kara were waiting at the usual meeting spot outside their homeroom. They both walked to school, so they usually got there before Jo. Emily usually arrived either first or last, depending on what time her father had to get to his job as a teacher at the high school. He dropped her off on his way to work.

"Hi there, party girl," Taylor greeted Jo. "Are you totally excited about your sleepover?"

"I know I am!" Kara said before Jo could answer. Kara always talked fast. She had four talkative brothers, so she had to be fast and loud if she wanted to be heard.

Jo reached into her backpack. "I'm definitely excited," she said. "I spent almost two hours last night making lists."

"Lists?" Taylor wrinkled her nose. "What kind of lists?"

Kara laughed. "For my first sleepover, the only list I made was how many ways my brothers would ruin the party."

Jo remembered that sleepover. Kara had been terribly worried about her brothers playing practical jokes on them. But in the end, the girls had turned the tables. They had played a big practical joke on the boys. It had ended up being a great party.

"That's not really true," she reminded Kara. "You had a list of things to do too, right? You had us make popcorn and watch DVDs and play games."

"I guess." Kara shrugged. "But I didn't write that stuff down or anything."

"Me neither." Taylor grinned and reached over to poke Jo in the shoulder. "But this is Jo Sanchez we're talking about, remember? She even organizes her sock drawer."

Jo smiled as Taylor and Kara laughed. She was used to her friends teasing her about liking things orderly and planned out. That was okay. She knew they were only joking, just as she was when she teased Taylor about being distractible or Kara about always being hungry.

"So do you want to see my plans or not?" she asked her friends. "I can always keep them secret." Now *she* was the one

teasing *them*. She knew they would want to know what she had planned for their next sleepover.

"Give it here!" Kara cried, grabbing Jo's notebook out of her hand. She flipped it open and peered at the top of the first page. "What's this?" she asked. "It looks like you crossed something out."

Jo took back the notebook and looked down at the page. "That's where I want to write the theme of the sleepover," she said.

"But I can't decide what it should be."

Just then Emily came hurrying down the hallway toward them. She dodged around some boys from their class who were kicking someone's lunch bag around like a soccer ball.

Emily made it past the boys and reached her friends. "Hi, you guys," she said in her soft voice. "Are you talking about the sleepover?"

"Of course," Taylor said. "We were just trying to think of a good theme for it."

"Do you have any ideas?" Jo asked Emily. Emily was the best of any of them at coming up with creative stuff like spooky stories or names for people's new pets. Jo figured she would probably be good at coming up with party themes too.

"Hmm, let me see." Emily dropped her backpack at her feet and leaned against the wall. Then she reached up and twisted a strand of her long, light blond hair around one finger. She always said doing that helped her think, even though it didn't make much sense to Jo. When she tried twisting her own hair around her finger, the only thing she could think about was how tangled her hair was getting.

"The first thing I thought of was having a spelling-bee theme, since that's why I get to have the sleepover in the first place," Jo said.

Kara looked worried. "No way," she said. "I don't want to spend our sleepover thinking about spelling. It's bad enough I have to think about it during school!" She shuddered. "Why do we need a theme for a sleepover, anyway? We never had one before."

"Sure we did," Emily pointed out. She was still twisting her hair thoughtfully. "Taylor's first sleepover was to celebrate the beginning of summer. That was the theme. The others all had themes too. We just didn't call them that."

"Ooh, I know!" Taylor said. "Jo's party could have a sports theme. Oh! Or how about a soccer theme? That would be cool. We could play soccer and make cookies that look like soccer balls or something."

Jo knew that Taylor loved sports, especially soccer. But Jo wasn't that interested in soccer herself.

Kara giggled. "This is supposed to be *Jo's* party, not yours, Taylor," she said. "If Jo was going to do a sports theme, it would be tennis." She glanced at Jo, suddenly looking worried again. "You're not going to make it a tennis party, are you? I'm not very good at tennis."

"I don't think so," Jo said. "I still think it should have something to do with the spelling bee."

"No, it shouldn't," Kara protested.

Suddenly Emily stood up straight and clapped her hands. "Yes, it should!" she cried.

"What?" Kara cried. "No way! I'm not spending all night spelling!"

"Hush, K," Taylor ordered. "I'm sure Emmers doesn't want to do that either. Let her finish."

"I'm not talking about a spelling theme," Emily said. "But the sleepover is partly because of the spelling bee, right? The *Spring* Spelling Bee."

Jo's eyes widened. "I get it," she said. "You think the sleepover theme should be Spring?"

"Right." Emily smiled. "Maybe something

like Welcome to Spring. Or how about Spring Has Sprung?"

"I love it!" Taylor clapped her hands. "Spring Has Sprung! That sounds like a totally fun theme."

"Definitely." Kara looked much happier now that they weren't talking about spelling anymore. "We could decorate cookies and cupcakes with spring-colored frosting, like pink and yellow . . ."

". . . and play Spring Tag," Taylor added. "It would be like TV Tag, but instead of naming TV shows, you have to name spring stuff."

"And for dinner we could eat spring foods, like fresh peas and spinach," Emily said. "I could bring them from my mom's garden."

Jo turned to a fresh page in her notebook and reached into her bag for a pencil. "I'd better start writing all this down," she said.

At that moment the school bell rang. All up and down the hallway students scrambled for the classroom doors.

"Too late," Taylor said. "Come on, we'd better get into homeroom before we're marked late."

Once she was sitting at her homeroom desk, Jo opened her notebook again. She wanted to be sure to write down all their great ideas before she forgot any of them. At the top of a new page she wrote SPRING HAS SPRUNG in big block letters. Then she started listing all the ideas her friends had suggested out in the hall.

"Hey, what are you writing?"

Jo glanced up. Max Wolfe was standing by her desk, staring down at her notebook. He leaned over to see what she was writing, but she covered her list with her arm.

"None of your beeswax," she said. Max was a big pain in the neck. He was always teasing all the girls in their class.

Max laughed. "I know," he said. "You're probably practicing your spelling. We should call you Spelly Sanchez!"

"Shut up, Max," Kara said from across the aisle. "Leave Jo alone."

Just then Randy Blevins wandered over. He was Max's best friend. "What's going on over here?" he asked Max.

"I said we should call her Spelly Sanchez. All she cares about is stupid spelling." Max pointed at Jo. "See? She's practicing her spelling in her spare time. What a nerd!"

"Spelly Sanchez! Spelly Sanchez!" Randy yelled. He was very loud. "Hey, Spelly, how do you spell 'nerd'?"

"Everyone knows how to spell that one," Taylor spoke up before Jo could answer. She sat right behind Jo in homeroom. "It's R-A-N-D-Y."

Just then the teacher came in to start

homeroom, and the boys hurried off to sit down. Emily leaned over toward Jo. She sat in front of Kara.

"Don't let those boys bother you," she whispered. "They're stupid."

"I know," Jo said with a smile. "And don't worry. I have better things to think about than them. Like our sleepover!"

# ✳ 4 ✳

## Strange Behavior

On Thursday morning Jo was excited to get to school and talk to her friends. She and her mother had made a shopping list the afternoon before. Mrs. Sanchez had even called Emily's mother to see what fresh spring vegetables she could buy from her for the party.

After her weekly clarinet lesson, Jo had worked on her list of games. Then, after dinner, she had made a list of ideas for decorations. By now she had three whole pages full of lists and notes in her note-book. She was sure her friends would love all her ideas.

Usually Jo was a very patient person. But today she barely waited for the bus to stop before she jumped out of her seat and hurried down the aisle.

"Where are you going, Spelly?" Max called out. He rode the same bus as Jo. "Are you in a hurry to get to homeroom and practice your spelling?"

Jo ignored him. She hopped down off the bus steps and walked past Randy, who was standing there waiting for Max. Then she headed straight inside.

Her friends were already at their meeting spot today. She could see them from halfway down the hall. They were standing close together. It looked like they were whispering to one another.

Jo walked faster. She didn't run, since the school principal was standing right there by the front doors. Running in the halls wasn't allowed.

"Slow down!" Principal Lewis called out loudly. For a second Jo thought the principal was talking to her, even though she wasn't running. Then she saw Max and Randy skidding past her. They were half-walking and half-running.

"Out of our way, Spelly!" Randy yelled as they rushed past and into homeroom.

Jo was almost to her friends by now.

They all looked up when they heard Randy yell. Then they stopped talking and backed away from one another.

"Hi, you guys," Jo greeted them. "What's up?"

"Nothing!" Kara said quickly. "Nothing at all. Nope, absolutely nothing."

"Ssh." Taylor nudged Kara hard with her elbow.

"Ouch!" Kara yelped.

Taylor smiled. "Sorry." Then she looked at Jo. "What she meant to say is, what's up with you?"

"Yes," Emily said, looking worried. "What's up with you today, Jo?"

Jo frowned a little. Her friends were acting kind of weird. But she didn't worry about it for long. She was too excited to share her plans.

"I wanted to show you guys my lists," she said. "The Spring Has Sprung theme gave me lots of great ideas." She smiled at

Emily. "My mom loves it too. She thinks we can get a tulip-shaped cake from the bakery. Get it? Tulips grow in the spring."

"That sounds cool," Taylor said. She looked over at Kara. "Doesn't that sound cool, Kara?"

"Totally cool," Kara agreed. Then she giggled, even though no one had said anything funny.

That was a little strange. But not *too* strange. Kara always giggled a lot. And she loved cake.

"Mom had another great idea," Jo said. "She thinks we should make a big banner to hang in the front hallway. It can have my name on it, and 'Spring Has Sprung,' and also my winning spelling-bee word."

She looked at her friends to see what they thought of the idea. Taylor was looking at Kara again. One of her eyebrows was raised, and her lips were pursed. Kara looked back at her, then covered her mouth quickly. But another giggle came out anyway.

"What's the matter?" Jo asked them. "Don't you like the banner idea?"

"We love it," Taylor answered. "Great idea. Definitely."

"Yeah," Kara added. She giggled again. "Definitely."

Jo frowned. She glanced over at Emily, who was being quiet. "What's wrong with them?" she asked.

"Who?" Emily asked.

"What do you mean, 'who?'" Jo waved one hand at Taylor and Kara. "Them. Why are they acting so weird?"

Emily shrugged. "I don't know what you mean. They always act weird." She laughed, then checked her watch. "Hey, shouldn't we go into homeroom soon? We don't want to be late."

"Let's go!" Taylor agreed. She grabbed

her backpack off the floor and scooted into the classroom. Kara and Emily were right behind her.

Jo followed more slowly. She was pretty sure she wasn't imagining things. Her friends weren't acting like their normal selves. What was going on?

The bell rang just as Jo sat down at her desk. All around her, other kids were setting down their backpacks and sliding into their seats. Her three friends all looked very busy putting their backpacks away. None of them looked over at her.

Jo looked down at her desk. She noticed several words written in pencil on its wooden surface. At least they were sort of like words. Most of them were spelled wrong. The words were SMARTY PANTZ, SPELUNG BE, and NURD.

She heard snorts of laughter from nearby. Looking up, she saw Max and Randy watching her.

"What are you reading, Spelly?" Max called.

Jo didn't answer. But this time it wasn't because she was trying to ignore the boys. This time it was because she was too upset.

She wasn't upset about the boys' silly prank. She was sure Max and Randy were the ones who had written the misspelled words on her desk. That was the kind of thing they were always doing.

But their stupid pranks didn't bother her. What bothered her was the idea that had just popped into her mind. It was a theory about why her friends were acting so weird all of a sudden.

Jo started rubbing the words off her desk with her eraser while she tried to figure out if her theory could be right. The more she thought about it, the more sense it made. After all, the boys hadn't started calling her Spelly until after the spelling bee. Just like Jo's friends hadn't started acting strangely until after the spelling bee.

Could her best friends be jealous of her big win?

## ✳ 5 ✳

## Keeping Secrets

Jo thought about her theory all morning. She tried to figure out if it could be true. She thought about how smart Emily was, and how well she always did in school. It was probably hard for her to watch Jo win, when she was just as good a speller.

Then there was Taylor. Taylor loved to win. She hated when anyone beat her at soccer or running or most other sports.

Maybe she hated losing the spelling bee too. Even to one of her best friends.

Kara probably didn't care at all about not winning the spelling bee. But she was the type of person who got excited when other people were excited, and sad when her friends were sad. Maybe she got jealous when others were jealous too.

*Yes,* Jo thought as she sat in math class. *I think this could explain why they're acting so weird.*

She decided to talk to her friends at lunchtime. There was no point in trying to ignore the bad feelings. They needed to talk about what was bothering them right away so they could go back to planning their sleepover.

Jo waited until the four of them were sitting at their regular table in the corner of the cafeteria. Then she took a deep breath.

"Listen, you guys," she said. "Are you upset about the spelling bee?"

Taylor looked up from unwrapping her sandwich. "What are you talking about?"

"I'm talking about this morning. You three were acting weird." Jo looked straight at Taylor, then turned to look at the other two too. Kara stared back at her, her big hazel eyes looking confused. Emily was gazing down at her lunch with her long, straight blond hair hiding half of her face.

"Weird?" Kara said. "What do you mean? We weren't acting weird."

"Yes, you were," Jo said. "But it's okay. I think I figured out why. You're upset because I won the spelling bee and you didn't."

Taylor laughed. "What?" she exclaimed. "No way. We're totally proud of you, Jo-Jo!"

"Yeah." Kara giggled. "What makes you think I even want to win a spelling bee? For one thing, if I did, everyone I know would probably pass out from the shock."

She sat up a little straighter. "Hey, that includes my brothers. Maybe next time I *should* try to win."

Emily reached over and squeezed Jo's hand. "We're all happy for you, Jo," she said. "Really."

Jo could tell she meant it. Emily wasn't a very good liar. Whenever she tried to lie, her lips quivered and her expression got all funny. She was pretty sure Taylor was telling the truth about not being upset too. When Taylor was really upset about losing a soccer game or something, she stomped around and acted grumpy.

"Okay," Jo said. "So then why were you all acting like weirdos this morning?"

"We weren't," Kara said quickly. "You must have been imagining it."

"Or if we were," Taylor put in, "it was probably because, um, right before you got there, Randy and his stupid friends were goofing off and acting like jerks."

"Yeah!" Kara's face lit up. "That's probably it. You know what jerks they can be. We were just, like, upset or something. Probably."

Emily didn't say anything. She suddenly seemed very busy sticking her straw into her juice box. Her hair was hanging over her face again.

"Oh." Jo wasn't sure what else to say. She could tell her friends weren't telling her the truth now. The trouble was, she wasn't sure what to do about it. She'd never had that sort of problem with her best friends before. Usually they told one another everything.

*Well, not always,* she thought as her friends started talking about something else. *There was the time Taylor didn't tell us she was afraid of spiders. And the time Kara didn't tell us her brothers were making her be their servant.*

Then she shook her head. Neither of those times were the same sort of thing. For one thing, neither of those secrets had stayed secret for very long. Besides, both of those times it had been one of them keeping secrets from the other three. This time it was all three of the others keeping a secret from her.

Jo didn't cry very often, but she felt a little like crying now. What could her friends be keeping from her? Why wouldn't they tell her the truth?

For the rest of the day Jo couldn't stop thinking about her problem. No matter how hard she thought about it, she couldn't figure out what was wrong.

There was only one thing to do. She had to try talking to them again. She decided she would do it after school. Usually they all hung out together for a few minutes before Jo had to get on her bus and Emily went to meet her dad.

After the final bell rang, they all wandered out toward their usual spot near the front doors. "Hey, you guys," Jo said. "I want to talk to you about something."

"Sorry, Jo-Jo," Taylor said. She looked at her watch. "It will have to wait until tomorrow. I have an early soccer match tonight, so I need to hurry home."

"Me too," Kara said. She giggled. "Um, I mean, not about the soccer match. But I need to get home early to, um . . ."

Taylor elbowed her. "You told me you have to rush home to feed your neighbor's cat," she said. "Remember?"

"Oh, right." Kara giggled. "He's always hungry."

"I told my dad I'd wait for him out front today," Emily added softly. "I think he's in a hurry too."

"Oh." Jo shrugged. "Well, I guess I might as well go get right on my bus, then. See you tomorrow."

"Bye!" her friends called as they hurried off. "See you tomorrow, Jo!"

Jo sighed as she watched them go. Then she went and got on her bus. Almost none of the other kids were there yet, so she sat down in a seat by herself near the front. She pulled out her notebook and opened it on her lap to her party-planning page. The list of party decorations was almost finished, though she still needed to work on the list of spring-themed games and activities.

But she couldn't concentrate on that.

Her mind kept returning to her friends and their weird behavior.

*I know,* she thought as she stared down at her lists. *Maybe I should make a list for this problem too.*

She got out a pencil and turned to a blank page. At the top she wrote BEST FRIENDS ACTING WEIRD. Then under that she wrote THEORIES.

Then she wrote #1: JEALOUS ABOUT SPELLING BEE.

She thought about their talk at lunch. She tried to remember everything the others had said. The more she thought about it, the more certain she was that theory #1 was wrong. So she crossed it off.

Next she wrote down a few more theories: THEY DON'T LIKE ME ANYMORE and I'M IMAGINING IT ALL and FRIENDS IN BAD MOOD TODAY. She thought about those for a while, but she wasn't sure they made sense. She even wrote down FRIENDS TAKEN OVER

BY ALIENS. That one made her laugh. It sounded like something Emily or Kara would think up. She crossed it off the list right away.

Then she sighed and looked around. A few other kids were climbing onto the bus by now. Max hopped on board with another boy. When he passed her seat, he stuck out his tongue at her.

"What're you doing, Spelly?" he asked. "Are you trying to write down every spelling word there is?"

The other boy, a second grader named Robby, laughed loudly. "Yeah, school's over, Spelly!" he cried. "You can stop writing stuff down now."

Jo ignored them as they pushed and shoved each other toward the back of the bus. They had just given her an idea for another theory, and this one made a lot more sense than any of the others. . . .

# ✳ 6 ✳

## A Dramatic Moment

As soon as Jo entered the school building on Friday morning, she spotted her friends. The three of them were in their usual spot. Once again they were leaning close together, whispering to one another.

Jo didn't hesitate. This time she was sure she'd figured out why they were acting so weird. And she was ready to do something about it.

She marched down the hall. "Hi," she said.

The three of them stopped whispering immediately. "Oh hi, Jo," Kara said. "And bye, Jo. I was just about to run to the bathroom."

"I need to leave too," Emily said. "I have to go get a book from the library before homeroom."

"Wait!" Jo said before they could move. "Don't go anywhere. I need to talk to you about something important."

Taylor bit her lip and glanced at Kara and Emily. "Really?" she said. "Um, can it wait till lunchtime? Because I need to—"

"No!" Jo said, not even letting her finish. "I've been thinking about it all night, and it can't wait. Especially since the sleepover is tomorrow."

"Oh." Kara shrugged, looking sort of nervous. "Um, okay. What?"

Jo took a deep breath. She knew what she had to do. Reaching into her backpack, she pulled out her notebook.

"Are you showing us your lists again?" Taylor asked, wrinkling her forehead.

Jo didn't answer. She opened her notebook to the pages of party plans. Then she ripped them out.

"Why did you do that?" Kara asked.

"I'm doing what you guys want," Jo said. She hesitated for only a second, looking down at her neatly printed lists. Then she ripped the pages right in half.

Emily gasped. "What are you doing, Jo? Those are your sleepover lists!"

"This doesn't mean the party is canceled, does it?" Kara cried.

"Nothing like that, don't worry," Jo said. "I just wanted to show you that I realized what was wrong."

"What was wrong with what?" Taylor looked confused as she stared from Jo to the ripped pages and back again.

"With my party plans." Jo waved the pages in the air. "I finally figured out why you guys were acting so weird. I've been treating this sleepover like a school project or something instead of a party." She shrugged. "I know you guys aren't like that. That's why you keep teasing me about my lists. You wish we could have a regular, less planned, more relaxed type of sleepover, like usual. So that's what I'm going to do."

All three of them just stared at her for a few seconds. Even Kara was silent for once.

Emily was the first one to smile, then giggle. "Oh, Jo!" she exclaimed, reaching out to touch the ripped pages. "I can't believe you just did that. Ripping up your lists was . . . was . . . well, it was like something *Kara* would do!"

Kara started to giggle too. "Yeah," she agreed. "I must be rubbing off on you, Jo."

"Maybe you're rubbing off on her a little," Taylor said. "But she's still our Jo-Jo. Otherwise she wouldn't even have all those lists to rip up!"

"True," Emily said. "But don't worry, Jo. We like you that way—honest!"

Kara nodded. "We're looking forward to our totally planned and organized sleepover."

"We'd expect nothing less from you," Taylor put in with a grin.

Jo blinked in surprise. She stared at Taylor, then at Kara, then at Emily. All three of them were smiling or laughing. Finally Jo smiled too.

"Really?" she asked. "So you weren't annoyed with all my lists?"

"No way," Taylor said. The others shook their heads too.

Jo was relieved. She was willing to have whatever kind of sleepover her friends wanted. But it had felt terrible to think that they didn't like the way she was planning it. After all, she was just being herself. She liked to be organized and make lists. It was a part of her personality, just the way liking sports was part of Taylor's, loving animals and books was part of Emily's, and being talkative was part of Kara's.

"I still can't believe you ripped up your lists," Kara said.

"We can help you rewrite them at lunch if you want," Emily offered.

Jo smiled. "That's okay," she said, tucking the ripped pages into her backpack. "I have the whole thing saved on my computer at home."

The others all laughed. "That's our Jo!" Taylor cried just as the bell rang to summon them into homeroom.

"Come on," Emily said, grabbing her backpack and slinging it over one shoulder. "We'd better go in."

Kara was still giggling. "Ripping up that list was definitely the biggest surprise of the week," she said. "Unless there's an even *bigger* surprise coming at the sleepover."

"No way," Taylor said instantly. "This is Jo we're talking about, remember? She plans everything—no surprises."

Jo was already turning to head into the classroom. She paused and glanced over her shoulder to add a joke of her own.

But she bit back the words. She was just in time to see Taylor poking Kara in the arm. Kara was grinning back at Taylor, rolling her eyes. Emily was chewing her lower lip and staring anxiously at both of them.

Jo's heart sank. She was glad that her friends weren't upset about her lists and plans. But she realized she still had no idea what their secret really was.

# 7

## A New Plan

"Excuse me, you guys," Taylor said, pushing back from her seat at the lunch table. "I need to go to the bathroom."

"Okay," Kara said.

Taylor leaned over her. "Don't you need to go too, K?" she asked.

Kara quickly swallowed the bite of chocolate-chip cookie she was chewing. "Oops!" she said. "I forgot. Um, I mean, yes. I do have to go."

She hopped up from her seat. Then she

and Taylor hurried off across the cafeteria toward the restrooms.

Jo narrowed her eyes and watched them go. "What was that all about?" she said.

"What?" Emily seemed to be very busy rearranging the lettuce on her sandwich. She didn't look up at Jo.

Jo sighed. "Never mind."

All day it was the same thing. Every time Jo convinced herself there was nothing going on, she caught her friends whispering or trading funny looks or doing something else that made her think there *was* something going on. But what was she supposed to do? She'd asked them about it several times already. If they didn't want to tell her, she couldn't make them.

After school Jo had to stay behind for a few minutes to ask the teacher a question. When she stepped outside, she saw her friends whispering together. As soon as she joined them, they all found reasons to rush away.

"See you tomorrow, Jo-Jo," Taylor said as she hurried off.

"Yeah," Kara called back over her shoulder. "We can't wait for the sleepover!"

Emily giggled, then bit her lip. "Um, bye," she said. Then she scooted away toward the parent pick-up area.

Jo stood there alone for a moment before walking slowly toward her bus. Suddenly, she wasn't looking forward to her sleepover at all. What if her friends acted this way all through it? If they did, it wasn't likely to be much fun at all.

*The best thing about the Sleepover Squad is hanging out with my best friends,* she thought. *But right now they're not acting much like friends at all.*

She stopped short, struck by a terrible thought. Max Wolfe was walking right behind her. He bumped into her.

"Hey!" he said. "Watch where I'm going, Spelly."

He hurried around her and raced toward the bus. She didn't move, or even notice him. She was too busy worrying over her terrible thought.

What if her friends didn't want to be best friends with her anymore?

She shook her head, not believing it

could be true. The four of them had been best friends since kindergarten. They would always be friends. Wouldn't they?

Just then the bus engine started up with a roar. Jo began walking again. Her feet automatically took her to the right bus, up the steps, and down the aisle to an empty seat. But her brain wasn't paying attention to where she was going. She was too busy trying to figure out whether her horrible idea could be true.

Jo felt a little bit better when she climbed out of the car at the tennis club. She loved everything about her tennis lessons. She loved the neat, clean white skirt, top, and sneakers she wore. She loved the fancy red and silver racket her aunt and uncle had given her for her last birthday. She loved figuring out how to hit the ball at exactly the right angle to skim over the net. She loved the weird way tennis players kept score—not zero-one-two-three like most sports, but love-fifteen-thirty-forty. And she loved the five other kids in her lesson. All of them except for one went to Birch Bark Elementary on the west side of town, so the only time she got to see them was at tennis.

"Hi, Jo!" Maureen Caldwell called when Jo hopped out of her mother's car. "What's up?"

"Nothing," Jo said, even though that wasn't really true. It would just be too complicated to explain what had been worrying her all day.

Marie Torelli laughed. She was the only other kid in the lesson who went to Oak Tree Elementary with Jo. "Jo's just being modest," Marie said, swinging her racket back and forth. "She won our school spelling bee this week. She beat all the fourth and fifth graders!"

"Wow, that's cool, Jo." Lanie Miller

smiled at her. "Congratulations. I was in our spelling bee last month, but I messed up on the very first word. Totally embarrassing!"

Jo giggled. "What word was it?"

Lanie rolled her eyes. "I can't even remember. I think I might have fainted after that."

That made all of them laugh. Lanie was one of those people who was really funny even when she wasn't saying anything that silly. It made her a great person to be around.

The other girls continued to talk and laugh. But Jo wasn't paying attention anymore. She'd just had a great idea.

*Maybe I should invite a few extra people to my sleepover,* she thought. *Just in case.*

She looked around at her tennis friends. All of them were nice and lots of fun. Jo had been to birthday parties at several of their houses, and she always had a good time.

If Marie and Lanie and the others came to her party, it wouldn't matter what Jo's best friends did—even if they decided not to show up at all. Jo knew it wasn't very likely that her best friends wouldn't come to the sleepover. But she wasn't sure how likely it was that they would be acting normal again by then.

Jo smiled. It was the perfect plan. She knew she should check with her parents first, but there was no time for that. It was already Friday afternoon, and the sleepover was tomorrow. She was sure her parents would understand.

"Hey," she blurted out, right in the middle of a funny story Lanie was telling about her older sister. "Do you guys want to come to my sleepover?"

# ✳ 8 ✳

## Phone Frustration

Lanie was the first one to answer. "A sleepover?" she said. "That sounds like a blast. But I already have plans on Saturday. Sorry!"

"That's okay." Suddenly, Jo thought of something. "Hey, how did you know it was Saturday? I didn't tell you that yet."

Lanie laughed and tapped her tennis racket against her leg. "Oh, yeah," she said. "Well, sleepovers are always on Saturday, right?"

"They could be on Friday," Marie pointed out. Then she smiled at Jo. "Sorry," she said. "I wish I could go. But I'm visiting my grandparents this weekend."

The other girls spoke up too. It turned out that all of them already had plans for Saturday night.

"No problem," Jo said. She was disappointed, but not that surprised. After all, she hadn't given them much notice. A lot of kids had things to do on the weekends.

Besides, her tennis friends weren't her only other friends. . . .

As soon as she got home from her lesson, Jo went to the phone in the two-story front foyer. Her mother kept a little green notebook beside the phone, where she wrote down the numbers of everyone she called. Jo flipped through it to the section labeled CHURCH PEOPLE.

She smiled as she dialed the first number. Her choir friends were just as much fun as her tennis friends. She was sure some of them would want to come to her sleepover.

By the time she hung up a half hour later, her smile had disappeared.

"This is crazy," she muttered as she checked the list once more to be sure she hadn't skipped anyone. She hadn't. She had called every one of her choir friends. And none of them could come to her party either!

Jo wasn't sure what to do next. She thought about calling her older sister and brother for advice. But they were both off at college in another state. She wasn't supposed to call them from the regular phone—only from her father's cell phone, which had free long-distance minutes.

She set the phone down and stared at it. What was going on? She was starting to wonder if she had any real friends at all. A few of her choir friends had sounded weird when she'd invited them — like they weren't sure what to say at first. But in the end, all of them had said no.

Then she thought back to her tennis friends. A few of their answers had been a little strange too. Like Lanie saying she was busy before she even knew for sure when the sleepover was going to be.

Jo was confused by it all. What in the world was wrong with everyone? Why didn't anybody want to come to her sleep-over? Even her best friends didn't seem that excited about it. In fact, Jo wasn't sure she was that excited about it herself anymore. Maybe it would be better if she canceled the whole thing.

She wandered across the foyer and into

her mother's home office. That was where Mrs. Sanchez ran her business. She went to yard sales and thrift shops and bought china and knickknacks. Then she sold them for a higher price on the Internet. Today she was busy wrapping up a pretty rose-colored plate in tissue paper.

Mrs. Sanchez smiled when she saw Jo. "There you are, Jo," she said. She set down the plate and brushed off her hands on her pants. "I was just going to come see if you want to help me get dinner ready. Your father should be home any minute now."

"Sure." Jo trailed after her mother down the hall and into the spacious, green-tiled kitchen. She could smell chicken baking in the oven. "Listen, Mom. About the sleepover . . ."

"Don't worry," Mrs. Sanchez said before Jo could finish. "I finished most of the shopping today. I'll just need to run out in the morning for a few last-minute things. Then I can help you with the banner and the other decorations."

Jo didn't get a chance to answer. At that moment her father came in shouting hello. Soon all three of them were sitting down to eat.

"How was your day, *mi cara*?" Dr. Sanchez asked Jo as he helped himself to some peas and carrots. "Do anything fun at school?"

"Just the usual." Jo was distracted. She stirred the vegetables on her plate, trying to figure out how to tell her parents she didn't want to have the sleepover after all. They had already made so many plans. She was afraid to just come out and say it.

"Are your friends getting excited about the party?" her father asked cheerfully.

"Sure, I guess." Jo cleared her throat, suddenly getting an idea. The reason her parents hadn't wanted her to host a sleepover for so long was because they didn't want their house messed up. If Jo reminded them how messy her friends could be, maybe they would decide to cancel the party themselves. "Um, Kara says she's probably going to be extra hungry tomorrow," she said. "I just hope she doesn't laugh with her mouth full. The last time she did that, she dribbled tomato sauce all over the floor."

Her mother chuckled. "Oh, dear," she said. "Maybe I'd better pick up some extra carpet cleaner while I'm out tomorrow."

"That Kara is a character," Dr. Sanchez said. "Things are never boring when she's around, that's for sure."

Jo decided to try again. "I already told Taylor she's not allowed to play soccer in the house," she said. "I just hope she remembers. You know how hyper she is sometimes." She glanced around. "Mom, maybe you'd better put away your vases and figurines and all the rest of the breakable stuff around here."

"Don't worry, Jo." Mrs. Sanchez reached for the platter of chicken. "We'll take away her soccer ball when she comes in. That should keep my things safe."

"That reminds me," Dr. Sanchez said. "On my way home I passed a sign for a spring carnival at the community center. How about if I take you and your friends over there to start off your sleepover? The sign said they're having a soccer ball–kicking contest." He laughed. "Maybe we can wear out Taylor before she gets here."

"Sure, that sounds fine." Jo tried to sound excited about her father's suggestion. But she was glad when her mother changed the subject to something else.

After dinner Jo decided to try once more to figure out what was going on with her friends. She asked if she could use the phone to call them.

She tried Taylor's house first. Mr. Kent

answered and told her that Taylor was still at her soccer match.

Next Jo dialed Emily's number. But the line was busy. So was Kara's.

Kara's line was almost always busy. Her brothers liked to play online video games for hours at a time. But Emily's family didn't spend very much time on the phone.

*That means Kara and Em are probably talking to each other,* Jo thought as she set down the phone. *Probably about whatever they've been whispering about all week.*

She looked at the clock on the wall, trying to figure out how many hours, minutes, and seconds were left until the sleepover started. But it wasn't because she was excited—just the opposite. So far, this was shaping up to be the worst sleepover ever.

# 9

## Spelling Things Out

"Come on, Taylor!" Kara cried, clapping her hands. "Try again!"

"You can do it," Emily added.

Jo smiled as Taylor made a face. It was Saturday afternoon, and the four of them were at the spring carnival with Jo's father. So far, things seemed to be back to normal. But Jo still hadn't forgotten about her friends' weird behavior all week.

"Okay, I'll try one more time. But then I'm out of quarters." Taylor fished some change out of her pocket. She was playing the soccer ball–kicking game at the carnival. So far she had won two stuffed animals and a baseball cap. But she couldn't seem to win the giant stuffed panda she wanted.

"Hurry up and win, Taylor." Kara licked her lips. "Jo's dad promised us ice cream on the way home, remember?"

Emily looked at her watch. "Don't worry," she said. "We have plenty of time before we have to be back." She shot Jo a glance. "For the sleepover, I mean."

Kara giggled. "We know *exactly* what you mean, Em."

Jo frowned a little. Was it her imagination, or were her three friends trading a very strange look right now?

*I always thought Kara and Emily were the super sensitive ones,* she thought. *Not me. I must be going crazy.*

Taylor didn't win on her next kick. But Dr. Sanchez gave her some more quarters, and finally she won the panda. "Whoo-hoo!" she cried as the game worker handed her the huge stuffed animal. "Isn't he cool? I think I'll call him Peter. Get it? Peter Panda!"

"I just hope we can fit him in the car," Jo commented. "I still don't see why we couldn't drop off the sleeping bags and stuff at home before we came."

"Waste of time," her father said. "We didn't want to miss anything here. Right, girls?"

"Right." Kara giggled. "We're on a schedule."

Taylor and Emily giggled too. But Jo just frowned. She didn't see what was so funny. And she still didn't understand why they couldn't have dropped off her friends' things after her father picked them up. All those suitcases and sleeping bags made the car awfully crowded.

She forgot about that for a while once

they made it to the ice cream parlor. Her father bought them all cones with any two flavors they wanted, and for a little while the four girls laughed and kidded around with one another just like always. Jo started to wonder if she really was just imagining that something was wrong.

After they finished their cones, the girls all crowded back into the car. Jo sat in the front seat beside her father, with Peter Panda crammed in between them. The other three girls were in the back.

For the first few miles everyone talked about the carnival and the ice cream they'd just eaten. Then, after a while, there were a few minutes of silence.

*The ice cream parlor was fun,* Jo thought. *Maybe this sleepover really will turn out fine after all. . . .*

Pushing Peter Panda's big fuzzy head aside, she glanced back at her friends. She was just in time to see Emily lean over something in her lap. Then Emily scribbled something on it with a pencil she was holding.

For a moment Jo was confused. Then she saw Emily pass the thing she was holding to Taylor. It was a piece of paper. They were writing notes to one another!

Jo gasped. "Okay, that's enough!" she cried, suddenly feeling fed up with the whole situation. "What are you writing? What's going on?"

Three sets of startled eyes stared at her. Taylor's greenish gold eyes looked startled. Emily's blue ones looked worried. And Kara's hazel ones formed perfect round circles as she stared at Jo.

The first person to answer was Dr. Sanchez. "Here's your answer, Jo," he said with a chuckle. "Look—we're home."

Jo hadn't even noticed that they had reached her subdivision. She looked out the window as the car pulled into her driveway, and her eyes widened to match her friends'.

"Oh my gosh!" she cried.

Hanging over the front door was a big banner. Red letters spelled out CONGRATU-LATIONS, JO! Just below that was the banner she and her mother had made featuring her winning spelling-bee word. People were pouring out of the house and

waving. She spotted her mother, her aunt and uncle, and Grandpapa Sanchez. Right behind them were her older brother and sister. She also saw some of her neighbors, kids from school, and all sorts of other familiar faces.

"Whew!" Kara cried from the backseat, clapping her hands. "I'm glad we're here. I couldn't keep that secret for one second longer!"

Taylor laughed. "Yeah," she said. "I think Jo-Jo was about to beat us up to get us to tell."

"Surprise!" Emily exclaimed. "It's a party to celebrate you winning the spelling bee, Jo!"

For a moment Jo couldn't speak. Her cheeks grew hot as she remembered how angry she'd been with her friends. She should have known they wouldn't keep secrets from her without a very good reason!

"Look," she exclaimed. "There are Lanie and Maureen from tennis."

Her father nodded as he turned off the car. "Your pals from choir are here too," he said.

"So that's why none of them said they'd come," Jo murmured to herself. "They didn't want to give away the surprise."

"What was that, *mi cara*?" her father asked.

Jo shook her head. "Never mind," she said. She waved to her brother and sister. "I can't believe Lydia and Al are here!"

"They didn't want to miss it," her father said. "They both came home from college last night and stayed over with friends so you wouldn't know they were here. We wanted this whole thing to be a big surprise."

"Don't worry, it was," Jo said. "Come on, let's go say hi to everyone."

She spent the next half hour talking to the party guests. It seemed as if everyone wanted to hear her spell her winning word. Jo must have spelled "choir" at least two dozen times.

Finally, she met up with her three best friends in the kitchen. They had all just helped themselves to sodas.

"So did you like the surprise?" Emily asked Jo, sounding a little worried. "We weren't sure you would."

Jo smiled at her. "I love it," she said. "But I can't believe I didn't guess what was going on! You guys aren't very good at keeping secrets, you know."

Taylor laughed. "Yeah," she said. "Kara's the worst."

"Hey! I'm not the one who almost gave it away at the carnival," Kara protested. "That was you, Em."

Emily giggled. "I guess we're lucky a super smarty like Jo didn't figure it out," she said. "She must have been too busy making lists for the sleepover."

Jo smiled. She didn't tell them how worried she had been all week. It didn't matter. The important thing was that everything had turned out just fine in the end.

"Hey, that reminds me," she said. "Are you guys still staying over tonight after everybody else leaves?"

"Of course!" Kara replied. "Even I know how to spell our favorite word: s-l-e-e-p-o-v-e-r!"

## Slumber Party Project:
## Fun and Games

Looking for some cool games to play at your next sleepover? Try one of these party classics.

WHISPER DOWN THE LANE: Everyone sits in a long row. The first person in line whispers a sentence to the next person. (Hint: Something a little bit long and complicated makes things more fun.) Then each person whispers the sentence they hear to the next person in line. But they can only say it once—no repeats. When the sentence reaches the far end, that person says what they heard out loud. Chances are it won't sound like the same sentence at all!

TV TAG: This is a variety of Freeze Tag. When the person who is "it" tags someone, that person must freeze in place. Anyone else can unfreeze that person by tagging them while yelling out the name of a TV show. Each show name can only be used once per game. (You can also try Movie Tag, Book Tag, Animal Tag, or any other category you can invent.)

MOTHER MAY I?: One person is "Mother." Everyone else stands in a line facing her. Mother then picks someone and gives her an order. For example: "Jump up and down three times" or "Touch your toes." That person must ask, "Mother May I?" before performing the task. If she forgets and just goes ahead and does it, she's out. If she does it right, Mother picks someone else and gives her a different order. Again, the person must ask, "Mother May I?" before following the order. (This game is harder than it sounds!) The last person left is the winner and gets to be Mother for the next round.